STARS FOR CRISTY

STARS
FOR CRISTY

By Mabel Leigh Hunt

ILLUSTRATED BY

VELMA ILSLEY

J. B. Lippincott Company

PHILADELPHIA AND NEW YORK

jH916st

CHAPTERS

1. CRISTY

*C*RISTY ROMANO paused dreamily at the exit of the neighborhood library. In her mind she was still poring over printed pages, reading of the girls and boys who live between book covers, yet who seem as real as life itself.

But the roar and clatter of the street brought Cristy out of her dream. And suddenly a sense of all her blessings seemed to spring up within her and dance for joy. It made her toes tingle. She eyed the distance between herself and the sidewalk. Then, clearing the three steps in one wide leap, she landed so lightly that the borrowed books under her arm scarcely shifted.

"Look where you're going!" A passing boy dodged out of her way. "Flying out like that you could knock somebody flat!" He glared at Cristy.

"Excuse," she said, and smiled at him. His ill humor had not clouded her joy in the least.

For it was the first really hot day of summer. *Summer*—it lay ahead of Cristy in a dazzling procession, one day after another, each as full of crowded action as Finney Street itself.

Cristy thought about the coming summer days. Momma Romano would say to her, "This morning my helper has worked like cement mixer. Now she may please herself." Then Cristy would most likely go to Dexter House, the social center on the Avenue. If the paved courts behind the building were not too blistering hot, Cristy might practice basketball or tennis with other children. She could swim in the big pool whenever a guard was present. Or, she might decide to play quietly with a table game. Dexter House was certain to start a new class in arts and crafts. Cristy might enroll.

But there would be times when she would far rather stay at home and play with her darling brother Salvadore. At the thought of fat eight-month-old Dory, Cristy's heart swelled with love and pride. She stumbled over a broken place in the sidewalk, dropping one of her books.

As she picked it up, she knew that books were also among her blessings. It would take a lifetime to read all she wanted to. Even then, she might not be through. But this summer she could surely read as many as ten books.

Not more than fifteen minutes ago, in the quiet of the neighborhood library, Cristy had entered "Summer Reading Adventure." Mrs. Rozell, the children's librarian, had shown Cristy the big poster mounted on one wall. It was shaped like an open book. The ruled double pages were blank, waiting for the names of young adventurous readers. The book was only a drawing. But it had meaning. Cristy thought it was both clever and beautiful. It reminded her of the great Book of Life which Momma Romano said lies forever on a golden table just inside the gates of Heaven.

"The Book of Life has names of everybody on earth," declared Momma.

"Our names, too?" asked Cristy, her spine prickling.

"Every name Romano," vowed Momma. "Your poppa and momma, your brother Nick, your little sister Carlotta and your baby brother Salvadore. Your name—Cristina Maddalena, plain as the sign on the Chinese laundry. The name of Bruno Torelli, your half brother who is nineteen and a sailor, God help him

All names of everyone on Finney Street, everybody on the Avenue, everybody in city. After the names old Saint Peter makes marks, good ones when we do right, bad ones when we do wrong. We should what-you-call 'watch our step,' or at the end of living we have all bad marks. Understand your momma, Cristina?"

Cristy understood. It was the same at the library. Mrs. Rozell had written Cristy's name on the big poster book. At the end of summer there would be a row of ten little gold stars after her name, one for each book she had read and reported on.

Mind busy and feet skipping, Cristy passed the Chinese laundry, the dry cleaner's, and Muggsy's Grill. Without a sidewise glance, she skipped past the second-hand shop and Ciello's fruit-and-vegetable stand. On the drugstore corner she halted, watching for a chance to cross the intersection. North and south, east and west, the streets roared with traffic.

As she waited, Cristy heard her name called. She turned. It was Marie Azarello, who lived in Cristy's block. Marie was carrying her swim suit in a plastic bag. Her wet hair lay as close to her head as a sealskin cap, black and shining.

"Hi, Cristy," Marie repeated. "You been to Dexter House today? I've been. My first swim since school let out. It was super. There's a new poster up at Dexter. Wiggsy is starting a new class."

"What kind of a class?" Cristy inquired.

"*Baby Care.*" Marie grinned, and gave her plastic bag a playful toss.

"C'm on. Now's our chance." Cristy snatched Marie's hand. Together they darted across the street.

"Don't ever think the class in Baby Care is for grown-up women," Marie resumed at the opposite curb. "It's for girls.

Gee whiz, Cristy Romano, does Wiggsy think we don't know anything? Haven't I helped my mom take care of little kids since I was six? There's Bertha Goldberg. What doesn't she know about looking after her mom's twins? There's you, with your Dory you're so crazy about. There's Ann O'Bannon. Well, there's all of us, nearly, with kid sisters and brothers we help take care of, and some of us plenty fed up with it, sometimes. If you ask me, Dexter House has about run out of ideas. *Baby Care!* I'd rather swim."

"It does seem a little queer to be teaching us that," ventured Cristy, thoughtfully.

Marie flashed a dark look at her. "Don't anyone dare say a word to me against Wiggsy and Dexter House!" she cried. "Maybe I did make a little fun just now. But it's different than you think. Baby Care is going to be taught like the books say, like the trained nurses know. Scien—"

"Scientific," Cristy finished. Listening and thinking, something warm and lovely stole into her heart. "What age girls may take lessons in Baby Care?" She asked it, cautiously.

"The poster tells, and to make sure, I asked Wiggsy," gossiped Marie. "The classes are for girls from eleven to sixteen. I'm twelve," Marie boasted.

" 'Eleven to sixteen,' " echoed Cristy. "I'm eleven." She almost sang it. *Eleven, eleven, eleven*—just old enough to enroll in a Baby Care class!

"I asked more of Wiggsy." How Marie loved to explain! "Wiggsy says that in the beginning the girls will have a big doll to practice on. At the last, when we know the rules, we shall use a baby out of the day nursery."

"A real live baby!" Cristy laughed. A star began to glimmer

in her mind, a star so faint and far away that perhaps it never would light up Cristy Romano's world.

Marie rattled on. "Wiggsy said that the teaching of Baby Care is part of the Settlement's home training courses. She said it will be useful whether a girl is just a big sister, or hires out as a baby

sitter, or when she grows up and has kids of her own. Any time, now, if I get the chance, I expect to baby-sit. Even if I do think the classes are a bit of a joke, I intend to get something out of them for myself. And that's a little money, some day. Cristy, why don't you enroll?"

Cristy studied her own two feet, bobbing up and down on the pavement as she trotted along Finney Street. "I don't know yet if I will, or if I won't," she murmured.

"Well, g'bye then," said Marie, airily. She ran up four steps, and entered a doorway. For a moment Cristy could see her sandaled feet springing up the stairs that led to the fourth-floor walk-up flat where the Azarellos lived. It was exactly like the Romano's flat three entrances east, for it was one of the many apartments of this block-long building called the Angel Flats. No one knew why the tenement had been given such a heavenly name. It was a great dingy pile of bricks, darkened by age, weather and soot.

Cristy, gazing through the dim entrance at Marie's vanishing feet, spoke to herself. "I wouldn't join the Baby Care class just to get something for myself. I'd do it because I'd love it."

It was now past mid-afternoon. Many women of the Angel Flats had left their hot apartments for a breath of air. They had time to loaf and gossip before cooking supper. They crowded steps and sidewalk. Others leaned sociably from windows. Their children called to the skipping young figure. "Hi, Cristy!" They waited for the glance she always flashed their way, quick and friendly.

Mrs. Harlovich shouted from her third-floor window. "Cristy! You better get a move on! In Number Fifty-One is a surprise."

Fifty-One, that was the Romano flat.

"Good surprise, or—or—bad?" asked Cristy, looking up.

"Good little surprise," chuckled Mrs. Harlovich. "Good, good." Her head bobbed with every "good."

Cristy squeezed past the women packed on the steps at her entrance. By their merry glances she was certain they also knew of the surprise in Number Fifty-One. The Angel Flat dwellers knew everything about one another.

Cristy bounded up the first flight. Up the second flight, not quite so fast. At the top she paused for breath. There was yet another flight before she would reach Number Fifty-One. Even a skinny eleven-year-old cannot tear up three flights of stairs at full blast. Not even when there is a "good little surprise" waiting for her.

2. SURPRISES

*B*UT there was something besides being winded that caused Cristy to halt at the third floor. She had to debate a question with herself. Of course she was eager to see the little surprise. The Angel Flat women would have known if it were a new swim suit or a pair of sandals which Momma might have bought for Cristy at the dime store. The surprise could be something about lovey-dovey Dory. Everyone around knew that Cristy regarded Dory as *"the* dish."

If the surprise had to do with Dory, might it not keep Cristy at home for a day or two? And how could she wait to see for herself the poster advertising lessons in Baby Care for girls from eleven to sixteen? It had taken Cristy a long time to become eleven.

From her stand in the hall, Cristy could see into Mrs. Harlovich's flat. That good lady still sat at her window, broadbacked, her gaze on the street below.

"I'll leave my books just inside Mrs. Harlovich's door, where they will be safe," Cristy decided. "If she wonders, she can see they are mine by my library card."

Cristy's slim legs twinkled down two flights. She dashed west for four blocks, turned a corner, ran north on St. James Street, and came to the Avenue. In the middle of the first block to the west, stood Dexter House.

Cristy flew up the steps, into the lower hall, and stopped, panting for breath, beneath the bulletin board. Tacked on its cork

the Romanos, especially Nick, believed it would not be too long before Bruno would command a flagship, in a uniform glittering with many breath-taking decorations.

"It is nice that Bruno is coming, Momma," agreed Cristy, this summer afternoon. Privately, however, she didn't consider the news as delightful as that Dory had cut his first tooth. "But I shall have to wait before asking Momma if I may study Baby Care at Dexter House," said Cristy to herself. "Now she is too excited about Bruno to pay attention to me."

"You notice Carlotta playing on sidewalk?" asked Momma. "Then run down and get her. She's been on the street long enough. You could read to her from one of your books."

"Oh, Momma!" complained Cristy. "I must hurry and win my first star. I can go twice as fast, reading to myself. Anyway, Lotta's too young for these books I borrowed."

"Hush, Cristina Romano!" Momma scolded. "Are you that selfish? Carlotta's only six. Maybe she doesn't understand all the words you read aloud, and what they mean. Listening, I don't always, myself. But they hang themselves up in our thoughts, Carlotta's and mine, and shine for us."

"Why, Mom!" Cristy gazed up at her mother in wonder. Words, sentences, and meanings—all the magic of books—shining in the mind. Momma Romano could read very little English, yet sometimes she could say pretty things like that.

"So now you read to Lotta and your old stupid mom?" coaxed Momma.

"You're not stupid!" cried Cristy. "You're wonderful! Mom, you will listen while I read to Carlotta?"

"I'll listen if I can keep my mind from July, when my Bruno will come home." Momma chuckled.

3.   A SECRET PLAN

*D*URING the next three days, while Cristy waited for Momma's excitement to simmer down, she finished a library book and won her first star in Summer Reading Adventure. In the meantime, Momma told Mrs. Harlovich about Bruno's coming. She told the Azarello's, the Goldbergs and the O'Bannons. Soon everyone in Angel Flats had heard. Momma told Catalona, the import man on the Avenue. She told Father Norman, and three of the Sisters at St. Agnes's.

Poppa tipped off his fellow workers at the shoe repair shop, and customers he chanced to see at Muggsy's Grill.

Naturally, Nick told Ciello the fruit-and-vegetable stand owner. He was helping Ciello this summer, part time. Nick broke the news to a dozen boys on Finney Street. He could scarcely wait for Bruno to appear in his jumper and funny-shaped trousers, his jaunty cap and winsome sailor collar.

As soon as her world knew that Bruno was coming home, Momma settled down to a radiant waiting. All she had to do was to shine up the flat, get a pile of mending off her hands, and as the time drew near, to cook some of Bruno's favorite dishes. She would make the finest of pizza pies. She would bake a certain Italian cheese custard Bruno had loved since childhood. Momma chuckled over her mending.

Cristy saw that Momma was in a quiet happy mood. Surely it was time for talk. She stood by her mother's chair, watching the big darning needle weave a web across the hole in Poppa's sock.

"Mom," Cristy began, carefully, "at Dexter House they're going to have classes for girls eleven to sixteen. I'm eleven, Mom. I could join up."

"What new notions the Settlement got this summer?" Momma smiled tolerantly.

"Baby Care, Momma!" cried Cristy. "Miss Downing, the regular nurse, and a nurse from the baby hospital will teach girls how to wash and feed and bubble and dress and sleep a baby. First a big doll, then one of the day nursery babies. Mom, it will be the *most!*"

Momma dropped her mending. She stared at Cristy. "We got a baby of our own, ain't we?" she snorted.

"Sure, Mom. But in the classes I would learn baby care the book way. By rule, Mom."

"Rule!" scoffed Momma. "Books! Haven't I raised five children without books and rules? If Cristy Romano wants, she can learn plenty baby care from her own momma. She doesn't have to be tearing off so nervous, washing dolls and other people's bambinos. Cristina Romano, afternoons you read library books and win those gold stars. Mornings you stay home and help your momma and read to Lotta."

"I do help, don't I, Mom?" asked Cristy, downcast.

Momma laid her mending on a nearby table. She drew Cristy into her lap. "Momma's helper!" she crooned. "Momma's good girl!"

Being rocked in Momma's lap was rare and charming. Cristy lay quiet, hating to break the spell. Yet time was passing. She lifted her head and began again.

"My friend at Dexter House thinks it would be awfully nice if I'd join the class." How proudly Cristy said *my friend!* "I

mean my friend Miss Pat Logan. Mom, I'd go two mornings a
week for four weeks. That's eight lessons. I'd get a little diploma
with a big gold star on it like I got for sewing last summer. I'd
be a better sister to Dory. Maybe some day I'll do baby-sitting.
I'd be a better baby sitter. I'd earn money, Mom."

Momma raised her eyes to the diploma Cristy had won for
sewing. Poppa had framed it proudly and hung it over a broken
place on the wall. "Always my Cristina is working for stars,"
mused Momma. "But summer is for a girl to rest and play
and swim and read and get fat." Suddenly Momma shoved
Cristy off her lap. "Get my coin purse out of the sugar bowl.
Run to Avenue and buy a bottle olive oil at Catalano's." Hands
on hips, Momma looked gravely at Cristy. "Girl, you keep shut
of begging for those lessons in baby tending till your momma's
had a chance to turn it over in her mind."

"Okay, Mom," sighed Cristy. She went out the door, clutching
the purse.

Momma Romano listened for a moment to the dragging feet
on the steps. She lifted herself heavily from her chair to lean
from the street window. Her gaze searched the groups of playing children below. "Carlotta Romano!" she shouted. "Come!"

Carlotta's six-year-old legs were short. It took her a while to
climb so many steps to Number Fifty-One.

"Wash those dirty hands, and that dirty face," commanded
Momma. "Cristina's gone to buy a bottle olive oil. Your momma
must climb to roof to haul in Dory's wash and have a little think.
Stay in flat, Lotta, and take good çare of bambino. I won't be
long."

Other women of the Angel Flats hung their washings on the
roof. But Momma was glad when she could have it to herself.

Up there the roar of the city seemed a little less. Above the crowding roofs, jutting walls, and rising chimneys, the little patch of empty sky seemed peaceful. Today, as Momma hauled in Dory's rather dingy underclothing, she was alone, and thinking.

It was several minutes before Mrs. Harlovich popped up through the hatchway to string up her own bit of wash. "Fine day on the roof, Mrs. Romano? Fine day for making white the baby squares?"

"But the soot from all around!" Momma complained. "Even in summer the washing can't be white like snow. Did you hear the news, Mrs. Harlovich?" Momma flashed a beam of pride at her neighbor. "Did you hear how Dexter House is giving school this summer in baby tending? My Cristina is going to join up."

"Momma!" Cristy bounded through the hatchway just in time to hear Momma's decision. She threw her arms around her mother's waist. Then she danced across the roof.

"No wonder Cristina's thin!" laughed Mrs. Harlovich. "She's never still."

Cristina wasted no time in visiting Dexter House. At the desk she smiled up at her friend, Miss Pat Logan. "It's lucky you are here," she declared.

Miss Pat was a volunteer worker at Dexter House. She didn't come every day. Cristy adored her. She had flared up when Marie Azarello hinted that Cristy cared because Miss Pat's people had money and lived in a plush suburb.

"That's not the reason I like her," Cristy explained at home. "I didn't even really know it for sure. 'Tisn't because Miss Pat is a doll, either. 'Tisn't because her boy friend sometimes comes after her in his ritzy car. It's the way she treats me. It's her, by herself."

At the desk, Miss Pat now smiled down into Cristy's shining eyes. "The class may not be fun for everyone, Cristy. But I'm sure it will be fun for you." In flowing script, Miss Pat wrote: *Baby Care. Class 2. Cristina Romano, aged 11.*

It would be fun, and more. It would be more than winning a diploma adorned with a paper star. It would be—Cristy felt sure of it—a way to make a sudden lovely and secret plan come true.

But it would take help. It would take help from kind Miss Pat. Wiggsy, so strict, and Momma, so careful, would need to understand enough to say "yes."

4. SO-SHE-ATE-CHERRIES

*I*N the summer evening after supper, Nick had rushed off to Dexter House for a dip in the pool. When he returned home, he flopped down on the street steps with Momma and Poppa, Cristy, Carlotta and little Dory. Above the chatter of many people around them, Nick gave Cristy the message.

"Wiggsy left word at the desk for you to see her tomorrow. She has something to tell you."

"Something to tell me?" echoed Cristy. She stood up, her hand on her chest. "Me?" she repeated. "Whatever—"

"Wiggsy offered me the same thing," declared Nick, importantly, "but I turned her down."

"You turned Wiggsy down?" cried Cristy. She stared at her brother as if he had said, "I just slapped down a couple of tigers over on the Avenue."

"Maybe your job with Ciello is making you feel too big." Poppa turned a hard gaze on Nick.

"I was polite." Nick spoke hastily. "I said, 'Thank you, Wiggsy, but this summer I have a job, but thank you very much.' That's what I said. . . . But you do as you please, Cristy," added Nick.

"Do? Do what?"

"Won't tell." Nick grinned. "You gotta make up your mind your own self."

"You could've held off till morning to tell your sister," scolded

Momma. "All night her head will buzz. Could be she might work up a fever, stewing with questions. Me, too."

Poppa laid a kind hand on Cristy's arm. "Night's for sleep," he advised. "With sleep, night goes fast. Morning comes. Then you get the news. Take it easy, sister."

Morning came. Cristy held herself in until after Poppa and Nick had left the flat. "You're all smiles, Mom. Did Nick tell you?" she asked.

"Yes," answered Momma. "And it's nice. It's wonderful. You skip to Avenue now. Like a mouse you wait for Wiggsy-lady to tell you. Then say to her, 'It's okay with my momma. Very much okay.' As always to the Avenue, Cristina, be careful at the crossings."

Cristy knew how to be careful and yet to fly like the wind. She flew to Dexter House, and stood tongue-tied at the railed-in desk in the hall.

"You're here, Cristy," said Miss Pat. "Wiggsy is in her private office just now."

Cristy waited on the wooden bench near the desk. The minutes dragged, although brightened by the merry glances of Miss Pat.

Oops! Wiggsy was sailing into view. Cristy tried to still her restless hands and feet. "Like a mouse," Momma had cautioned.

Miss Pat spoke to Wiggsy. "The little Romano girl is here."

Wiggsy beckoned. "You know, Cristina," began Wiggsy, "that Dexter House furnishes children with vacations at our summer camp at Green Lake."

Cristy remembered. Only last year Nick had enjoyed a wonderful week at Green Lake.

"But we cannot always send everyone," Wiggsy went on.

"There are too many children, not enough weeks of summer, and not enough money."

Cristy nodded. "Too many children . . . not enough money." At Angel Flats and up and down Finney Street, she had often heard these clear explanations.

"But this year," Wiggsy went on, "Associated Charities has aroused the interest of some farmers up in Caspar County. The farmers have agreed to take children into their homes for a free country vacation of about two weeks. Associated Charities will pay for a simple new outfit of clothes, if necessary, and bus fare to and fro.

"You are one of the children we have selected for this treat, Cristina. You deserve it. It will do you good. You are much too thin." Sternly Wiggsy sized up Cristy's bones. "Well, Cristina?" demanded Wiggsy, in her crisp-as-celery voice.

Cristy gulped. "You mean a real farm, like in library books? You mean fields, trees, rivers, like in pictures? All that?" Cristy flung her arms wide. "You mean cows and chickens and—and maybe a horse?"

"These days farmers use tractors, combines, fertilizer spreaders, wheat drills and I don't know what all, or how they can afford so much machinery," stated Wiggsy. "But, well—a horse is possible."

"It's lovely up in Casper County," Miss Pat chimed in. "Wide and wonderful green space. Lots of sky, Cristy. Good things to eat. You will come back to us plump and brown."

"How shall I get there?" breathed Cristy. "On a long twisty train?"

"By bus. There will be a bus load of children."

"Nick told my momma," Cristy babbled. "Momma says okay I can go."

"Then make the entry, Pat," ordered Wiggsy. "Cristina Romano to the Todd farm on Route Two. The Todds want one girl. Here's the list of clothes you should have, Cristina. Tell your mother to buy only what is necessary, and nothing fancy. Bring the bill to me. I'll turn it over to Associated Charities. You must be here, washed clean with soap, Cristina, on Thursday, June twenty-first. The bus will be out in front, and will leave for Caspar County at nine. Is that clear?"

"Yes, Mrs. Wiggs. Thank you, Mrs. Wiggs." Never before had Cristy called the rock-of-ages at Dexter House anything save "Wiggsy." But now it seemed unholy.

"And please, will you thank So-She-Ate-Cherries for being so good to me and the other kids?" cried Cristy, out of a full heart.

"It's Associated Charities, Cristina," corrected Wiggsy. "It's a body, not a person."

So-She-Ate-Cherries—a kind, kind body! Light-headed, Cristy flew out of Dexter House. But on the Avenue, she moved by inches, studying the list Wiggsy had made. *Sweater. Swim suit. Jeans and shirt. Shorts and blouse. Sandals. Pajamas. Two sets underwear. Toothbrush and comb.*

"New everything!" whispered Cristy. "Travel! Maybe a horse when I get there! Please God, bless So-She-Ate-Cherries."

Cristy turned into St. James Street, walking tiptoe. She must go lightly. Her new happiness seemed so delicate as to be breakable. And a moment later it broke into pieces, shattered by a sudden reminder of the summer plans she had already made. She trudged back to the Settlement and up to the counter.

"Please, Wiggsy, I can't go on the bus."

"And why ever not, Cristy Romano?"

"I just remembered the class. I'd miss it. I couldn't miss Baby Care."

"Oh, for mercy's sake!" Wiggsy made a wry little face.

"Angel!" cried Miss Pat to Cristy. "For a minute you had us worried. The Baby Care classes don't begin for a month. You'll be back from the country long before that."

Cristy began to shine again, but almost as quickly clouded up. "I'm in Summer Reading Adventure," she said, chin down. "I have to read ten books."

"Cristina Romano, you are taking a great deal of our time!" exclaimed Wiggsy. "You have weeks to read ten books, and I'm sure the librarian will allow you to take one or two with you." From over her square shoulder Wiggsy turned a cool look on Cristy. "Once and for all, do you want a country vacation? Or—don't you?"

"Excuse me for being such a trouble," begged Cristy. "I do want to go very much, now that I'm sure I can do Baby Care and Reading Adventure. My," sighed Cristy, "such a rich summer!"

Wiggsy motioned Cristy out of her sight. But Miss Pat walked to the entrance with her. "Chum," she murmured, "you're so—well, I love you." She gave Cristy a quick, laughing hug.

Cristy floated homeward on sidewalks which might have been feathers. The four flights to Number Fifty-One might have been clouds.

"Mom, Miss Pat loves me! Mom, I'm going to travel! Wiggsy has fixed it up with a rich, kind body named So-She-Ate-Cherries. I don't know her. Maybe I'll never see her. But she's paying my bus fare to the country. She's paying for my new clothes.

Here's a list you're to buy. Mom, maybe I'll ride a horse, like the girls and boys in stories."

"Only a little horse, my Cristina, gentle and slow. Don't you fly around on any racers!" Momma was saucer-eyed.

"I want to ride a horse!" wailed Carlotta. "I want to go to the country."

"Lovey, you're too little," soothed Momma. "And what would I do, with both my girls gone from me?"

Something forlorn crept into Cristy's heart. Saying good-bye. Being away from home for the first time. She leaned over the cooing Dory.

"Momma!" cried Cristy. "What if I couldn't bear to leave you and Dory and everybody on Thursday the twenty-first?"

"Hush!" Momma scolded. "This is fine chance you have."

5. OFF TO THE COUNTRY

*I*T was Thursday, the twenty-first. The city school bus trundled along the highway. Almost three hours ago it had left Dexter House. From the start it had been a rattlebox of noise. It's driver was Joe, a good-natured, steady sort. He was used to children bouncing around in a bus. Skilfully he had zig-zagged through the mazes of the city and its suburbs. He had driven through two thick-set towns, five strung-out villages, and some open country. An hour ago he had stopped at a village station to buy ice-cream cones and soft drinks for his passengers.

Most of the children neither knew nor cared who had paid for the refreshments. But Cristy Romano cared, and she knew. Amid the clamor she told her seat-mate, who happened to be Ann O'Bannon of Angel Flats.

"I saw Wiggsy give Joe the money," said Cristy. "Wiggsy is good."

"Of course," agreed Ann. "But I don't think it was Wiggsy's very own money." The vision of a large shadowy source of funds for Dexter House filled Ann's mind. Cristy's, also. "It could've been So-She-Ate-Cherries," she offered, thoughtfully.

"Who?" Ann demanded.

"So-She-Ate-Cherries, the rich, kind body that Wiggsy said was buying our clothes and paying our fares to the country."

"Doesn't sound right," Ann remarked.

Cristy was not going to argue about anything Wiggsy had told her as fact. And just then Joe shouted news and advice.

"We're coming into the county seat, where folks are to meet you and take you to their farms. Now's the time to show your manners. Don't let the farmers think that city kids are wild animals loose from the Zoo."

The rattle-box bus became almost as still as a country lane at dusk. Some of the children were suddenly pale and tense. Some were flushed and eager. What were farm people really like? What sort awaited this boy or that girl?

"*Todd*—that's the name of my folks. They *want* me!" Cristy comforted herself. Hadn't Wiggsy said, "the Todds want a girl?"

On the court-house lawn, names were read off. Ann O'Bannon left Cristy's side and walked away with a smiling woman and a rosy-cheeked girl. "Maybe the Todds will have a raft of children I can play with," said Cristy.

But when the Todds claimed her, they were alone. Ready and willing to like them, she did so, from the first. Mr. Todd took the string-tied paper box holding her clothes. Mrs. Todd carried the two library books, also tied with string.

Cristy had dreamed that the Todds would come for her on their riding horses, bringing an extra steed for her. But there were no horses. She rode between the farm couple on the front seat of their car. Above her head Mrs. Todd said, "I was kind of hoping we'd get a skinny girl. And we have! It will be fun to fatten her up."

They followed a black-top road, narrow and quiet. Wild roses and elderberry bush bloomed along the fences. It was strange to see so few people, so few buildings, no sidewalks, no shops, so much space. It was like being on another planet than the one in which Dexter House, Finney Street and the Angel Flats were so important.

"Maybe you could call me Daddy George while you're visiting," suggested Mr. Todd. "My first name is George."

Mrs. Todd laughed. "And mine is Eva. But you call us whatever you like when you know us better. We used to have a little girl. But now she's grown, and lives a long way off with her husband and baby. We miss her. That's one reason we wanted you. Tell us about your family, Cristy."

Nothing suited Cristy better just now than to describe the dear far-away people in Number Fifty-One, although it made a lump swell in her throat. When she came to Dory, she had to stop, trying to think how she might give the Todds even a hint of Dory's charms.

"His real name is Salvadore. He's eight months old, and borned his first tooth the other day." Cristy sparkled up at Mrs. Todd. "Dory is—he's beautiful. There's not—" Cristy was about to say there was no baby anywhere in the wide world so perfect. But after all, she couldn't brag like that.

"Little Salvadore must be cute," said Mrs. Todd. "Italian names—all of them," she added to her husband.

"We're Americans," declared Cristy. She went on to tell about Bruno, and how he happened to be *half*. "Bruno brags some, but not so much you can't like him," she confided.

"So? Well, here we are." Mr. Todd turned the car into a drive, and then into a neat garage. A lop-eared hound sniffed at Cristy's legs as she followed the Todds to the house.

"His name is Tomboy," explained Mr. Todd. "But now he's old, and the laziest hound in forty-eight states."

Well, even a lazy dog might be fun!

"See our lovely view, Cristy?" asked Mrs. Todd, as they paused on a side porch. She gave the child's thin shoulders a caress.

"We're so happy to have you, dear. We want you to feel at home."

Cristy's eyes wandered. There was no stopping place. Fields and woods and pastures—the wide country rolled away as far as she could see. Above curved the blue dome of the sky, vast and empty.

"It's nothing like home," she murmured.

"But you will love it," Mrs. Todd assured her.

"Mom said for me to take off this good dress the minute I got here. I'm to put on my shorts or jeans. Everything's new."

Cristy changed in a bedroom which was to be hers. It was neat and pretty. It smelled of soap and the sweet air floating in from the fields.

For dinner there was stewed chicken, gravy spreading over hot biscuits, tender vegetables, fresh jelly, apple dumplings with a rich sweet-sour sauce. Cristy ate and ate.

"Excellent dinner, Eva." Mr. Todd complimented his wife.

"I used extra butter," she confessed. "I intend to fatten Cristina. Then she will be downright pretty. In fact, I doubt if her baby brother will know her when she goes home again."

Cristy helped with the dishes. Mrs. Todd said that she and Mr. Todd usually took little afternoon snoozes. "I guess it's our big noon dinners that make us sleepy. A nap would be good for you, child. See that slat hammock under the trees? George made it in memory of the one he liked when he was a boy. It's comfortable for napping."

6. A STAR FALLS

*C*RISTY tried out the oddness of the wooden hammock. When she had learned to keep it from tilting her out, she lay back. With one foot she pushed herself idly to and fro. She had known she wouldn't sleep a wink, so she had brought a library book. Only farm people and a kitten like Dory took afternoon naps.

Brother-r-r! How astonishingly quiet! The Todds had disappeared. Even Tomboy the hound lay on the lawn as if dead. Time—it was something you noticed in the country. It did not rush headlong as in the city, on a million noisy feet, on a million grinding wheels, roaring with a million ear-splitting voices. In the country Time floated slowly and quietly, like that gleaming big cloud high above the slat hammock and Cristy Romano.

Ten days of slow, soundless time! Oh, the Todds were as kind as could be. But they were strangers, really. Their farm was astonishingly strange. Why had a city child come so far? Why had she come at all? Was Momma wondering this very moment about her girl, and perhaps worrying a little? In the shoe repair shop was Poppa feeling sad because he knew he wouldn't see Cristy for many suppers, for many breakfasts? Even Nick, sorting good fruit from bad—did he think of his sister once in a while? Was Lotta complaining to Mom that Cristy was not there to read aloud? And saints above—wouldn't darling Dory know Cristy when at last she returned so fat and changed to Number Fifty-One?

Cristy turned her face from the eye-like windows of the Todd farmhouse. Into the clean old quilt spread across the hammock, she wept lonely tears, and was ashamed of them. In the city she almost never cried.

Presently she fumbled blindly for her book. The bright little star she would win for its finishing, once she had returned to blessed Finney Street and the blessed library, twinkled faintly in

her mind. But she was obliged to read the first page several times before she could even begin to forget her longing for home. Mrs. Rozell had assured her that this was a good story. Cristy now discovered that while the heroine did not live in a place like the Angel Flats, she had thoughts and feelings which Cristy understood perfectly. While the bright cloud floated slowly above the farm, Cristy found comfort in a book. And *Boy!* All at once there galloped onto the pages a horse, a swift, slim-legged creature who was to become, Cristy felt sure, a close friend of the heroine.

Cristy sat up so suddenly that the hammock tilted and spilled her out. "I forgot to ask Mr. Todd if he owns a horse!" she recalled, scrambling to her feet. She studied the wide landscape, and rubbed her eyes, and looked again. By some country magic, had Cristy Romano become the girl in the book? For there, in a green pasture, was a horse! It was moving slowly, cropping grass.

Cristy whirled. She bounded toward the house. Where was Mr. Todd? But on the porch she pulled herself up short. A girl who has Mrs. Romano for a momma does not go barging into a strange house when everyone is asleep. But in her mind, Cristy was pleading, silently, "Wake up! Please wake up, Mr. Todd!"

And he did! He appeared at the doorway, rubbing the sleep from his eyes.

Cristy pointed. "Mr. Todd, is that—could that be *your* horse?"

"Sure it's my horse." The farmer chuckled. "Come. We'll visit him. We'll ride him over my land. But first we'll get a saddle."

The barn was topped with a saucy weathercock, but Cristy walked through the door with almost a church feeling. She had read about barns. This seemed to be a perfect one. There was a pleasant fragrance of hay and leather. The rafters were high and shadowy, and from the deeper floor shadows a cat's eyes gleamed greenly at Cristy before they disappeared.

"Abby the cat is a good mouser," said Mr. Todd. "Now here is the stall where my horse stays when he's not out grazing. Here are the stalls for our two cows. I used to keep a herd and sell milk and butter and beef. But not any longer. These days I go in for hogs and field crops." The farmer drew Cristy to the big open door. "See all those hogs out there, and their shelters? Once we had a young woman greenie visiting us. And Cristina, she thought the hog shelters were dog kennels! Wasn't that a joke on her?" Mr. Todd threw back his head in loud merriment.

Cristy laughed, pretending that she herself was no greenie and would know a hog shelter anywhere.

"In the big sheds, and all around the barnyard," Mr. Todd explained, "you see my farm machinery." He named them as he pointed them out. Cristy had read farm stories. But never had she come across any mention of wheat drills, corn planters and pickers, rotary hoes, hay balers and the like. The names were nothing but jargon to her. She was glad when at last Mr. Todd lifted a saddle from the wall. "Ready, go," he said. "And here comes Tomboy. That dog knows we're bound for Old-Timer's pasture."

On the way, Mr. Todd explained the horse to Cristy. "He's quite a young animal. But I named him 'Old-Timer' because it is definitely old-timey to keep a horse on a farm. Once in a while Old-Timer does a bit of work for me. But mostly I ride him around my land, and enjoy him. I'm a softie about horses, because as a boy I grew up with them on my father's farm. Do you like horses, Cristy?"

"I'll say!" Cristy was radiant. "I've read nearly all the horse stories in the library."

At the pasture gate Mr. Todd whistled. Old-Timer came cantering up. He nuzzled his master's hand. "Old-Timer, this is Cristina, the girl who has come to visit us," said the farmer.

Cristy dipped a bow. Old-Timer didn't bow, but he blew out his nostrils, softly. While being saddled, he stood perfectly still. "He can go fast enough for me when I give him the reins," boasted Mr. Todd, "but he's gentle and well-mannered. Later, it might even be safe for you to ride him alone."

Cristy had fancied she would leap to a saddle the first chance, and gallop away over hill and dale like the fearless boys and girls in books. But now she backed off. She couldn't help herself. She had not realized that a horse is so tall.

"You have two weeks to get acquainted with Old-Timer," Mr. Todd assured her. Before she quite knew how it happened, she was seated on that horse! The farmer was in the saddle, in front of her. How tightly she clung to him! Now they were off, first at a walk, then at a trot, and for a short while at a gallop. Bump, bump—Cristy had never been so thrilled and shaken up in her life. Wonderful So-She-Ate-Cherries—ah, she knew what she was doing, sending Cristy Romano to a farm where there was a riding horse! Boy! Wait until Cristy could tell Nick! Just wait until she told Wiggsy, Pat Logan, and Mrs. Rozell! Oh, for the big-eyed moment when she would simply stagger Marie Azarello and the other girls!

Cristy hardly saw the rich acres she crossed. She scarcely heard Mr. Todd's explanations. "Over there are my orchards, chiefly cherry and apple. In the rough land above are my raspberry canes. Here is our corn. It's tall for this time of year. Now, all of this is in wheat. We shall be harvesting next month. Yonder big field is in alfalfa. Away down there, where you see the line of trees, is the river."

"A river!" sighed Cristy. How often a river had flowed through a story she had read and loved!

"Now we'll follow the little path through my grove, then out to the road and home again."

Riding softly through the woods seemed beautiful. Cristy

didn't mind the stillness. She had a real live horse under her. The farmer was near, and talkative. Tomboy was good company as he snuffled bushes and dead leaves.

They left the woods. Old-Timer's hoofs beat a rapid tattoo on the grassy berm along the highway. Then he was walking up the driveway. Mrs. Todd hastened to help Cristy down.

"George," she said, "when you are back from taking Old-Timer to the pasture again, we shall have a snack. After that, it's my turn to show Cristy my flowers and vegetables."

As Cristy ate Mrs. Todd's fresh gingerbread washed down with milk, it seemed surprisingly silly of her to have felt such loneliness an hour ago.

She was thrilled with the vegetable garden. Would her fruit-and-vegetable brother believe her when she told of seeing peas and lettuce and new onions, rhubarb and strawberries, not in crates and bins, but growing by themselves out of earth?

And oh, Mrs. Todd's flowers! On the Avenue Cristy had often stopped to stare at blossoms behind glass, haughty lord-and-lady flowers which a Finney-Street child could never hope to touch. But here, in a country garden, were flowers within reach, heavenly fragrant and warm with sun. On every hand was gay friendly blooming in spikes of blue, in clusters of pink and white, in bells of purple, in rosettes of red. "If Carlotta could only see them!" breathed Cristy.

"While I fix supper you may pick nasturtiums for the table." Mrs. Todd pointed to the glowing borders. Oh, it was almost as wonderful as riding a horse. It was something Cristy would always remember. "Am I busy picking flowers!" she bragged to nosy Tomboy.

After supper, she was invited to help feed the chickens. It was exciting. As the birds crowded around her, she felt as free-handed as the great So-She-Ate-Cherries. It gave her a shock when Tomboy suddenly bounced into the midst of the flock. *Yoicks*— how he chased the cockerels and fryers and old hens! Such squawking and frantic scattering, such flurries of loosened feathers! Mrs. Todd gave Tomboy a hard slap. He trotted back to the house, tail lifted with pleasure. "That's Tomboy's favorite prank," explained Mrs. Todd.

She and Cristy did the dishes together. The kitchen was almost blinding with electric light. White enamel gleamed. Even the suds sparkled in the dishpan. Mr. Todd came in with the pails of milk. "You can't do everything in one day, Cristy," he joked. "Tomorrow, when I milk, I'll let you hold the cows' tails. But now evening is here. We'll sit on the porch and enjoy the cool night air." He turned out the house lights.

Following her host and hostess, Cristy shrank back at the sudden darkness which met her at the door. "Ooo-ooh!" Surprise shivered out of her. If she took another step, would not darkness grab her? Wouldn't Night carry her into black, mysterious country?

"Come, dear," coaxed Mrs. Todd. "I have brought out the small chair which belonged to my little daughter. Sit down. It's been a long day for you since leaving the city this morning."

This morning—so long, so long ago! Cristy sneaked out and groped for the chair. Skinny though she was, it was a tight fit. She sat tall and uncomfortable above the low back. Out there, in the deep shadows, *Anything* could plainly see Cristy Romano in the little chair. She drew in her feet. She tried to hunch smaller.

Away off, beyond the wide Todd acres, the lights of other farmhouses twinkled faintly. For Cristy they only made darkness and distance greater. Crickets sang in the grass. Cristy had never heard them before. She believed that the sound they made, so small and strange and creepy, was the voice of Night-in-the-country. Miserable, she shrank in the little chair. If somehow Momma could reach out through miles of darkness, and draw Cristy back to Number Fifty-One!

"Bedtime, Cristy!" At last Mrs. Todd made a cheerful stir. "Want to go out into the yard with me and look at the stars before going to sleep? I always do. It's then I say my prayers. The stars make me know that God *is*."

Cristy didn't wish to stir a step. But she walked out, clinging to Mrs. Todd's hand. They stopped where there were no trees, and turned their faces to the sky. "Oh!" gasped Cristy. "It isn't a planetarium, is it?"

"Dear no! Those are real stars up there. That's the way the sky looks of a clear moonless night. Isn't it splendid?"

Cristy gazed upward, spellbound. In the vast sky were millions of tiny bright lights. Some of them twinkled. Some burned with a steady fire. Across the zenith swept a path of glittering dust.

Cristy had never dreamed that a night sky could be so wondrous.

"Quick, Cristy! See that falling star?" Mrs. Todd's voice was charged with soft excitement. Cristy's spine prickled. Indeed she had seen a swift pencil of light slant downward across the sky.

"Where did that star go?" she whispered. She felt cold.

"I don't know," answered Mrs. Todd.

"Do stars fall on people?"

"I never heard of it." Mrs. Todd patted Cristy's shoulder. "Now come, for tomorrow will be a busy day."

From her bed near a window, Cristy could see the stars. Not the entire sky full, but so many that she turned her back to them and covered her head with the sheet. She lay tense, reciting her prayers, hot one minute, cold the next. What if a star should fall down through space to burst over Cristy Romano's bed in a bright, destroying rain?

Burrowing into her pillow, snatching at the sheet, Cristy prayed for daylight. "I can't stay on this dangerous farm another night. The city is safe. In the city there are no stars, except the little one Nick saw over Muggsy's Grill. But oh, what a shame! Now I shan't grow fat and maybe pretty. I can't pick any more flowers. I can't feed the chickens or hold the cows' tails. Now I shall never, never learn to ride Old-Timer all by myself, and I did want to see the river.

"The Todds will be sorry. They won't understand. They will think I'm just a bad-mannered girl. Wiggsy will be cross. And there's So-She-Ate-Cherries. Gee, she will think I'm 'chicken,' being afraid in the country. She will think I'm a cheat, wearing the new vacation clothes she gave me not even for a whole day!"

Cristy tossed and turned. The pillow slip became a moist wad.

7. THE RUNAWAY

*C*RISTY got up early the next morning. She was careful to move about on tiptoe. By the time she was called to breakfast she had made her bed. She had packed her clothes in the cardboard box and tied the string. She had tied up her library books.

At the table she felt jittery. She could scarcely eat, although kind Mrs. Todd kept urging. "Cristy looks a little pale," she said to Mr. Todd. "She may not have slept well her first night. Didn't you, Cristy?"

"Yes," fibbed Cristy, and dropped her toast, buttered side down.

"Well, anyway, you had better take things easy today," Mrs. Todd advised. "Play quietly with Tomboy, while George and I do a few necessary chores at the barn."

As soon as Cristy saw the Todds disappear into the barn, she fled to her room. Out she came, carrying her belongings. With an eye on the barn door, she hurried along the driveway. Now she was on the black-top road. Tomboy was bounding joyfully after her, believing he was to have a morning frolic.

Cristy came to a row of trees. They would hide her from view, in case the Todds looked her way. Now she whirled on the dog. "Go back, Tomboy, go!" she scolded. She pointed toward the house.

Tomboy paused, one foot lifted until he was sure he had heard aright. When Cristy commanded him again, he turned tail and trotted homeward. "It's queer," he might have said in

dog speech, "but I guess I know when I'm not wanted."

Up the road Cristy hurried. Now that she was really on her way, she was filled with happiness, although there were a few inches left within her for sharp regrets. "But Dory *will* know me," she assured herself. "I'm hardly a bit fatter."

It was early. This road was never heavily traveled. So far no cars had passed Cristy. But presently she thought she heard her name called. She turned for a quick look. No one was in sight. The call came again. "Cristy! Cristy! Cristy Romano!" It was not a voice she knew. It had a strange hollow sound, as if it held all of space within it, the wide country emptiness, the high blue reaches of the sky.

Now another voice called from a different direction. It came from far, far away. It was an echo. But Cristy didn't know that. What great ghostly voices could be calling Cristy Romano, who was only trying to escape another night of falling stars? From what far-off watchtower did an enormous *Somebody* see her, small and alone?

Cristy began to run. Her feet pounded the highway. Under her shirt her heart pounded wildly. She raced so fast that every breath became a pain. And just as she knew she could not run another step, the string broke which had tied her box. All her things tumbled out on the pavement.

Flushed and panting, Cristy knelt. She began to gather up the articles. But at least she could work in peace. For the voice which had called her had fallen silent. What a relief! In a moment, when she had retied the string and had recovered her breath, she would go on. She didn't know the way. But she would get there.

"Cristina!" The voice was deep and gentle. It was near. Cristy spun around. At the fringe of a grove Mr. George Todd sat astride his horse, Old-Timer. Cristy was quick to notice that the farmer did not look cross. Indeed, he looked even more kind than yesterday.

He dismounted. Leaving the well-behaved Old-Timer at the edge of the wood, Mr. Todd had Cristy's things collected and the box tied before she could draw her next painful breath. He led Cristy to the horse. Up she went. Up went her box and her books. Up went the farmer himself. He wheeled Old-Timer around. Mr. Todd and the runaway rode back through the grove.

It was Mr. Todd's own grove. The yellowing wheatfield which the riders passed was his. Cristy knew it, now. For all her running she had not even passed the borders of the Todd farm.

"We're having a sunset picnic by the river this evening, Cristy," began the farmer, quietly. "We're going to toast wieners over a fire. Eva planned it yesterday. While you and I were out riding, she phoned a girl we know, named Susan Reed. Eva invited Susan to share our picnic and to bring a young visitor of her own. The picnic by the river will be nice."

Cristy leaned against Mr. Todd. She was very tired. The silence he let fall between his quiet words was soothing. Presently he went on as quietly, but more gravely.

"You had neither food nor money with you, Cristy. The city is eighty miles distant. You do not really know the way. Something might have happened to you. It would have broken our hearts. What would your mother think, and the people who sent you to Caspar County, if they knew what you just now tried to

do? When we discovered you were gone, and had taken your things, we felt both sad and frightened. I called and called. All I heard was a faraway echo. I mounted Old-Timer. I rode across my land, hoping to head you off."

Cristy hung her head.

"At the farmhouse, when you are rested, we shall talk together," said Mr. Todd. "We shall not make you stay if you don't really like us and our farm."

" 'Tisn't that I don't like you," Cristy quavered. "I do, truly."

Mrs. Todd's face was like the sun when she saw them coming. She ran out, reaching high to lift Cristy down. For a moment she held her close. "Honey-girl," she whispered, "you will get over your homesickness. We shall have lots of fun, really! Come, wash your hot face and hands, and brush your hair. Here is milk and a sandwich." Food was the farm cure for almost every ill. Cristy did manage to choke down part of the offered refreshments.

"You feel better," beamed Mrs. Todd. "How would you like to help stem and sugar strawberries for our picnic this evening? Three happy girls and a boy playing by the pretty river!" Mrs Todd looked bright and eager.

Cristy gulped down her last bite. She would have to say it, now, right out, to the kindly Todds.

"The picnic would be nice," she began, in a low voice. "But after the evening, comes night. Oh, please, I must go home before another scary night!"

Mrs. Todd slipped her arm around Cristy. "Child, why didn't you tell me last night that you were afraid? And for mercy's sake, afraid of *what?*"

"Stars," whispered Cristy. *"Falling* stars."

Mrs. Todd couldn't speak for astonishment. Mr. Todd blew a soft whistle of unbelief.

"Don't you remember last night?" cried Cristy. "A star fell out of the sky. We saw it. You said you didn't know where it went. But it had to fall somewhere. This very night a star could fall from right up there!" Cristy pointed at the innocent blue sky of daytime. "You are brave," she went on. "But I am afraid. On Finney Street, where I live, there's never a star to fall on me. I must go back, where it's safe."

Mrs. Todd drew Cristy into her lap. "Mercy, mercy!" She repeated her "mercies" as if they pained her. Yet a little smile played around her mouth. "Dear child, listen to me," she began. "The stars are shining above us right now in millions, just as we saw them last night. We can't see them because it is day, and the sun making sky and world so bright. They shine in countless numbers above Finney Street, night and day. They do, Cristy! It is only because of the tall city buildings and the blazing city lights that you can't see them. Last night, Cristy, as we looked at them here in the country, I was thanking God for their everlasting glory. I was thanking Him that I had a little city girl— *you*—to gaze at them with me. I prayed that you would know that the stars are a part of the marvelous order and rhythm of our universe—day and night, Cristy, sun and stars, turn and turn about, every month, every year—forever. I prayed that our green fields, our wide sky, our flowers and fruits, the river, Old-Timer, the chickens, the cat and cows you scarcely know yet, our love for you—I prayed that all of these you would remember in the city with happiness."

Mr. Todd drew up a chair. He patted Cristy's hand as he talked to her. "There is change as well as everlastingness," he said, quietly. "Stars and mountains and seashores change. Men build new roads, new cities, new houses. They invent new things. Girls grow. They have new experiences, like going to the country for the first time, like getting acquainted with a horse, or gathering garden flowers. They read new books, and learn truths about life and people they have never known before.

"When we see a star fall, Cristy, we know it is because of some change in the life of that star. But the falling star is far, far away. It burns out as it strikes the air which surrounds our earth, before it can harm us. But because the lives of stars and mountains and seashores are very, very long, we call them everlasting. Try to understand, Cristy."

"Even if you don't fully understand, will you trust us when we promise that not a single star will fall on you while you are here?" asked Mrs. Todd.

Cristy gazed into the honest eyes of her hostess. She studied her kindly host. She slipped off Mrs. Todd's lap. Slowly she swung herself around one of the porch pillars. "I s'pose it was wacky of me," she admitted, pink-cheeked. "It was impolite." She stopped swinging. "But even with the stars not falling on me, even with you so good, I don't see how I can live without seeing my mom and Dory!"

"Oh," moaned Mrs. Todd, "how I understand! I remember being dreadfully homesick once when I was a child. But George, I did so want Cristy to stay! I declare, I'd keep her even if I—

"Cristy!" cried Mrs. Todd. "Don't stir off this porch. George and I have something to talk over in the house. Wait, dear! Wait!"

8 .   WISH I MIGHT

*C*RISTY sat on the porch, waiting. She felt definitely small fry, but also very mixed up. She was ashamed of being such a trouble to the nice Todds. She was ashamed of her lack of trust in them and in the everlasting stars. One part of her longed to stay on the farm. Another part of her, the Cristy of Angel Flats, longed for home and family.

Tomboy came to lay his head on her knee. She fondled his silky ears. How did the old hound know that Cristy was so troubled?

After a while Mr. Todd appeared on the porch again. "Cheer up, Cristy," he advised. "By evening, or at least by morning, we shall either send you home, or something will have changed your mind."

Cristy did feel rather cheered. But all through the noonday dinner she was timid. There were no after-dinner naps. "We'll sit on the porch and stem strawberries, Cristy, just in case we do go to the river, as planned." Mrs. Todd smiled as if she felt certain of the picnic. She went on. "Do sit down, George, and relax. Cristy, George is waiting for a telephone call."

Twenty minutes later the farmer was jumping as if the telephone had rung inside his head instead of from its place in the dining room. Cristy could hear his voice, but not his words. She was surprised when he called her, saying, "Some one you know will talk to you."

Cristy was not used to a telephone. Her hands were sticky

with strawberry juice. She took the receiver gingerly, and almost dropped it after uttering a shy "hello." For the loud response almost deafened her. Oh, she would know that voice anywhere! She felt weak with amazement and delight.

"My daughter, Cristina Maddalena Romano, yes? This is your momma from the drugstore booth on Finney Street. Cristina, I hear things from the farmer. He has kind voice. He says kind things about you on phone. But girl, how come you're not happy? Now say the truth loud to your momma."

"Oh, Mom," quavered Cristy, "the folks here are nice, awfully nice. Their farm is a storybook farm. I mean it has everything I've read about in farm stories, even a wonderful horse. I rode the horse, Momma, with the farmer. . . . But I feel bad, Mom. Not in my stomach, that needs a spoon with castor oil. It's only that I'm sick for you and Dory, and the others."

There was a little silence. Then again Momma's shouts. Was not the drugstore booth eighty miles from the farm? "Cristina Maddalena, it makes you feel better, hearing me?"

"It's wonderful, Mom."

"Then listen," shouted Momma. "I'm okay. Little Salvadore is okay. Carlotta lost a front tooth this morning. That's okay, too. It's Carlotta growing up. Poppa and Nick are fine. We're here, same as always. But we're there, too, on the farm with you. Our love is with you, the same as God's love. Remember that. . . . Cristina, what nice thing the folks plan for you today, maybe?"

"A picnic, Mom, by a real-for-sure river. A girl named Susan to play with me, and her visitor." Telling Momma about the picnic made it seem a jolly thing a child wouldn't want to miss.

"Girl, you go on that picnic," Momma advised at the top

of her voice. "You have happy time. Forget your Cristy-self. Think of the good farmer folks. Think of your Wiggsy-lady and all who give you treat. Think of Romanos, so happy you have fine chance. Cristina, save up in your mind and tell us about that picnic when you get home. Tell us about that horse. We sit around table and listen with our mouths open . . . . Cristina Maddalena, your momma loves you. But she has a little shame that you trot out sickness for home so soon. How long you been gone? Only since yesterday. 'T ain't giving farmers fair chance, or you, or anybody. Straighten up, girl. Hear? Your momma wants you to stay. She knows you'll be sorry if you don't. Lovey, you'll be good, now, and not have sickness for home any more?"

"I'll try, Mom." Cristy choked on the words. "I'll stay."

"Cristina, before I forget!" trumpeted Momma. "Did you see stars last night?"

"Yes, Momma."

"Sky full, like in Italy?"

"I—I guess so."

Momma's voice softened. "Cristina, nights you look at stars. It's beautiful chance you have. You think in your mind, 'When my momma was a little girl like me, she saw these stars in other land. Same wonderful stars, Cristina, same wonderful everlasting-ness. . . . Now we talk too long, maybe, for the farmer to pay for?"

"No!" cried Mrs. Todd, hearing every word. She sprang to take the receiver from Cristy. "Hello, Mrs. Romano. This is Mrs. Todd. Before you hang up, I . . . Cristy, run away. This is talk just between your mother and me."

Cristy had to run as far as the barn to get out of earshot of her mother's voice. There, it was necessary to shed a few tears. But it was also necessary to skip. Sometimes a girl can skip and cry at the same time.

Presently the Todds came to the side door. Cristy could see that they were beaming with pleasure. She ran to them. "Cristy Romano!" exclaimed Mrs. Todd. "Such a wonderful mother as you have!"

Cristy knew it. But—"did you tell Momma about me and the stars?"

"We wouldn't tell on you," answered Mrs. Todd. "But a mother like yours—she just knows, somehow. Come, Cristy, we'll pack our picnic baskets, shine ourselves up, load the car, and pick up Charles."

"Who is Charles?" inquired Cristy.

"You hadn't given yourself time to find out," Mr. Todd reminded her. "Charles is the son of my tenant, the man who helps with the farm work. See yonder house? That's on my land. That's where Charles Westover lives with his parents."

On the way to the river, Cristy and Charles sat in the back seat of the car, with Tomboy very important between them. A little more of her foolishness, and Cristy Romano would never have met Charles Westover. She liked him.

At the chosen picnic spot, the river had changed its mind and decided to become a brook. Shallow and clear, it sparkled over pebbles and sand. But while Mr. Todd built a fire and Mrs. Todd unpacked baskets, Cristy and Charles walked along the curving tree-shaded banks and saw how the stream became a river again, deep and brimming. Cristy was brimming, also. Cristy Romano, walking by a storybook river, a river that moved in poetry she had learned at school!

And here and there a foamy flake
Upon me, as I travel. *

Returning, Cristy and Charles heard laughter and gay chatter. Two girls and a woman had arrived. One was the girl named Susan. The other was her mother, Mrs. Reed. Who was the other girl? Cristy cried out in glad surprise. "Ann! Ann O'Bannon!"

"It's Susan's farm I'm visiting." Ann's tone was the same as if she had said, "It's heaven I'm visiting."

Cristy and Ann explained at such a rate their words ran together. "We both live in the Angel Flats. We're in the same school. We came out on the same bus yesterday, for country vacations. Isn't it funny we meet at the same picnic? Isn't it a scream?"

It was. The girls screamed. Charles, sharing the excitement, turned a handspring.

Ann drew a sharp breath when Cristy told her about Old-Timer, and that she had actually galloped miles—simply miles—on his back.

"By yourself?" cried Ann.

"Not yet," spoke up Mr. Todd. "But when I've had time to teach her, she may ride alone."

"We have a big pond on *our* farm," boasted Ann. "We have a boat. We row. I caught a fish this long!"

While the sizzling sausages sent forth mouth-watering odors, the children waded in the ripples. The water was cold and tickly on their ankles. At supper they stuffed themselves until they felt as fat as the wieners, and the same shape.

Charles told a story he had made up. It was crammed with

* From *Song of the Brook*, by Alfred, Lord Tennyson.

pirates, buried treasure, spaceships, ghosts and monsters. In the gathering twilight it could have been fearsome. Instead, it was so overdone that it brought forth screams of laughter. Charles

himself laughed so hard that no one could be sure how his story turned out, if at all.

"Oh, look!" cried Susan. "The first star!" She turned, so that she could make her secret wish over her left shoulder. It comes true if you do that, or at least it should.

> "Star light, star bright,
> First star I've seen tonight.
> Wish I may, wish I might
> Have this wish
> I wish tonight."

Cristy listened to Susan. Star and chant were new to her, and new to Ann. Each of them, and Charles, took turns chanting. The star shone like a little silver daisy in the pale evening sky. Cristy wished a big *something* for Dory.

The picnickers sang in the twilight, while the water sang, too, as it rippled over the pebbles. Darkness had fallen by the time everyone was at home again.

"If you like, Cristy," offered Mrs. Todd, "I will share your bed until you fall asleep."

Cristy shook her head, resolutely. "I'm not going to be a fraidy cat tonight. Not after all you and Momma told me."

Again Cristy stood on the lawn while Mrs. Todd said her nightly prayers. Again the sky was studded with millions of stars. Again it made Cristy's heart stand still, with its everlasting glory and mystery.

Cristy thought about her mother, once a little girl loving the Italian stars. She thought of Susan and Ann, of Charles and herself, hopefully making wishes.

Star light. Star bright.

9. TRICK STUNT
—AND A LETTER

*B*Y early rising, Cristy knew that her second full day on the farm promised the kind of happiness she had dreamed of. Feeling rested, and easy in her mind, she ate a hearty breakfast. She fed the chickens. How she loved them because they crowded around the feet of a stranger—herself! She helped with the dishes. She picked peas, the pods cool and plump in her fingers.

Cristy was determined to make friends with the cat. She prowled about in the barn, and after much coaxing, had Abby in her arms. Tomboy noticed at once. He planted jealous paws against Cristy and barked until the morning rang. The cat leaped away and up the nearest tree trunk. After some dainty tight-rope walking among the high branches, she settled down on a mere twig. She lay switching her angry tail, gazing down at Tomboy with eyes that glowed like live coals.

Cristy felt well enough acquainted with Tomboy to scold him. As it suited him to rest, anyway, he stretched out under the wooden hammock. Above his paws he watched to see whether the day would continue to be interesting.

No amount of coaxing could bring Abby from her lofty perch. Perhaps she couldn't get down. It is often easier to do a rash thing when one is excited and angry than it is to undo it. Cristy was relieved to see Charles coming.

"What shall we do?" she called with such helpless pleading that Charles felt equal to anything.

"Here goes! I'll have that old cat down in a jiffy," he promised. He spat on his palms, grabbed the tree trunk, and shinnied up.

"You're as slick as a city fireman." Cristy's praise gave Charles the strength of ten. He climbed higher than ever in his life, and within two feet of the cat. But stretch as he might, he could not reach her. She just lay there, blinking at him.

"Stubborn ninny!" Charles backed down the tree. "I'll fix her!"

"Never mind, Charles." Mrs. Todd came out with some meat scraps. "We'll set this plate at the foot of the tree," she said. "Abby will see it and smell it. In her own wise time she will come down, I hope. Charles, you're to take Cristy to the hay-field. Your father and George are raking this morning."

"I know it," answered Charles. "The only reason I'm not working my head off in the hayfield myself is because George said I was to show Cristy around." Charles was somewhat like a half brother named Bruno Torelli. Both bragged, but not so much that you couldn't like them.

Mrs. Todd disappeared into the house. As the children trudged toward the field, they looked back. And what did they see but old Tomboy gobbling up the meat scraps which were supposed to tempt Abby down from the tree! Cristy was shocked. But Charles thought it very funny.

"George said we can ride Old-Timer today," said the farmer boy.

"D'you know how?" gasped Cristy.

"I can ride any horse a-living, I guess."

Cristy felt honored to know Charles. But at the hayfield she

almost forgot his boast and the wonderful prospect of horseback riding. The haymaking was fascinating. She tried to understand Charles's glib talk about the side delivery rake, the hay baler and the bale loader. She tried to follow as he pointed and exclaimed: "See? That's how it's done. Now, watch it!" Finally Cristy felt it only fair to explain that she was not good in arithmetic.

"Holy smoke, what's arithmetic got to do with it?"

"I don't know exactly," Cristy admitted. "Machinery or something, I s'pose." She drew in deep breaths of air. The fragrance of the new-cut hay was heavenly.

Charles felt as high-nosed as a country squire showing his lands to a beautiful but dumb lady, while his servants toiled and sweated at the haymaking. Only, he couldn't feel that way more than a moment. He was, after all, a boy of eleven. The toilers happened to be his father who was a skilled farmer, and George Todd, owner of the field, the hay, the hay rake, hay baler, bale loader and wagon. Besides, the attention of Charles's lady was

not altogether undivided. She kept waving to George Todd. "What say we go and sizzle around on Old-Timer?" Charles suggested.

"Let's do," agreed Cristy. In her dreams had she not pictured herself on a horse?

Cristy only just made it when she and Charles mounted Old-Timer from a top fence rail. The horse was such a gentleman he might have picked her up and brushed her off had she failed to make a safe landing. As it was, he cantered gently off, having politely changed his plans for the day to please a couple of children.

"Isn't this wonderful?" screamed Cristy, as Charles dug his heels into Old-Timer's flanks, and increased speed.

"We can ride all day if we want to," Charles said.

"Oh, I do wish *people* could see me riding a real, live horse— trot, trot!" longed Cristy.

"What people?"

Cristy named several of her friends in the city. Ann was one of them.

"That's easy," Charles declared. "I mean, it's only a few miles to Susan's house. Ann is there. Bet her eyes will pop at sight of you riding."

Cristy squealed her delight. On the way she had the strange experience of going through a covered bridge. She had seen pictures. "I'm a pioneer girl, Charles. Take me through the bridge again." After Charles did so, she asked him when she might ride Old-Timer all by herself.

"D'you think you could?"

"Except for you, I'm doing it this minute!" declared Cristy, rattlebrained. "My, wouldn't I just love to gallop alone to

Susan's house, and have Ann see me? Charles, couldn't you pop off the horse and hide somewhere, pretending you're not around?"

Charles was not sure he cared to become nothing, even for a few moments. He was also doubtful about allowing Cristy to ride alone. "If you'd use your head, I guess there couldn't be any harm in it," he ventured. He could understand what fun the plan might be for her.

At a turn in the road opposite the Reed's large vegetable garden, Charles reined Old-Timer to a halt. He slipped from the saddle. "I'll hide behind this boulder. You ride on." The huge stone lay at the side of the road.

Cristy adjusted herself to what seemed like two or three yards of saddle. The reins felt very light and slim in her hands, and for a moment she felt alarm. "Giddup," she squeaked. Old-Timer also felt a natural alarm. And when Charles gave him a hard whack from behind, he leaped forward. Cristy's head jerked violently. Every bone and joint in her body seemed to rattle as Old-Timer galloped up the road. And the saddle—*bumpity-bump* —it was certainly no feather cushion!

Cristy could see the unfenced lawn in front of the Reed's house. On its far side was the driveway. She had noticed how Mr. Todd and Charles had shortened rein, left or right, in turning the horse. She must turn Old-Timer into that driveway when she came to it.

Tense with purpose, excited and unskilled, Cristy was also rushed by Old-Timer's belief that great speed was expected of him. She pulled on the left rein much too soon. The horse leaped a shallow ditch which Cristy hadn't even noticed until it suddenly yawned beneath her. Then Old-Timer bounded into the Reed's front lawn.

It was a lovely lawn, studded with beautiful shade trees. And as if it had been slyly waiting all its life to play a trick on Cristy Romano, a hanging branch hooked itself under the halter of her jeans as she sped beneath it. Old-Timer galloped on toward the farmhouse. But Cristy hung in space by her halter, legs dangling.

That is how Charles saw her as he peered above the boulder. That is how Ann and Susan saw her from the Reed's front porch, where they were playing.

"For heaven's sake, whose is the body?" Susan sprang to her feet.

Ann stared. "Looks like Cristy Romano!" The girls cast startled glances at Old-Timer, who had stopped at the house. They looked again at Cristy, then ran to her. Charles came tearing up from the road. The children tugged at Cristy's legs. They pushed her upward. Neither pushing nor pulling did the least good. The rascal bough was too high for them to reach. "Ow! Ow!" yelled Cristy.

"Help!" Ann turned wild eyes toward the farmhouse.

"Mother, come quick!" screamed Susan before she remembered that her mother had gone to Hicksburg on an errand.

It was Charles who had an idea, although not a very bright one. Rushing to the long-suffering Old-Timer, Charles drew the horse to the porch, flung himself into the saddle, and with careful aim, walked him up to the dangling Cristy.

Old-Timer was nervous. What was this object? If it were human, why was it thrashing about in such a position? The horse backed and wheeled, tossed his head and rolled his eyes. What a time Charles had to get him into position, and to stand still long enough for Cristy to drop onto his back!

When she did come down, sideways and with a thump, it

was somewhere between crest and withers. Old-Timer danced. But while Cristy clung, Charles yanked the hooking tree branch away. "Ouch!" wailed Cristy.

But she was free. Within minutes she was seated on the front steps. She let the halter strap of her jeans drop and turned to Susan. "Am I bleeding?" she asked.

"About to, in streaks."

"It burns like fire," said Cristy. "We'd better go home, Charles."

Charles couldn't think of anything he'd rather not do. He would be blamed for allowing a greenie to ride by herself.

As for Cristy, she was feeling a good deal smaller than ten minutes ago. But she regained her lost inches when Ann cried out. "Cristy Romano! From what you said at the picnic last evening, I thought you didn't even know how to ride. But here you are doing trick stunts already!" Ann gazed at Cristy with round, admiring eyes.

"Heck!" muttered Charles.

"I don't believe Cristy meant to do a stunt," objected Susan.

"But all the same, she did a stunt!" cried Ann. "It was neat, Cristy! It was super!"

Riding to the Todd farm behind Charles, Cristy felt puffed up by Ann's flattery. Her back and shoulders were scratched. She had been frightened. She had felt ridiculous, dangling helplessly from the tree. She had felt stripped of glory as a rider. But— after all!

Charles was silent and sulky.

"Could I help it if that old tree was right in my way?" Cristy demanded of his unfriendly shoulders.

No answer.

"Could I help it if that old tree reached down and snitched me right off Old-Timer's back?"

"Quit asking silly questions," growled Charles.

" 'T isn't every girl, Charles Westover," Cristy flared, "who can do a trick stunt like that on her very first ride alone." Yet Cristy had the sense to giggle at such a false boast.

"You know you're talking crazy," answered Charles. He let out a hoot that was supposed to drip with scorn. But almost at once it turned into real merriment. Charles laughed so hard he nearly fell out of the saddle. Cristy laughed, too. "It was silly!" She giggled. "It was the silliest thing that ever happened to me!"

Old-Timer wasn't used to such peals of laughter falling into his ears. Inside the covered bridge, where the sound bounced off the walls in shrill echoes, Old-Timer decided he'd had enough. He had a right to act a bit light-minded himself, also light-footed. Over the plank floors Old-Timer tap-danced from side to side. "Whoa, there, Boy. Behave yourself." Charles reined him in.

At the farmhouse, Mr. Todd was in from the hayfield. Dinner was ready. Charles must stay. He would far rather have ducked for home. But he would have been thought a sneak if he weren't there when the Todds saw the scratches on Cristy's bare shoulders.

"What happened?" cried Eva Todd, noticing at once.

The children explained.

Mr. Todd looked Charles in the eye. "Even a grownup needs to be taught to ride a horse. I had planned to start Cristy with some proper lessons late this afternoon. Eat your dinner, Charles Westover."

While Charles and Mr. Todd ate in silence, Mrs. Todd sponged and treated Cristy's scratches.

As Charles started dumpishly for home, Cristy called after him, "Thanks, Charles, for saving my life." He turned, grinning happily once more.

Cristy and Mrs. Todd then had dinner. "There will be no more horseback riding this day," said Mrs. Eva. "You had better rest."

After such a wild morning, it would be pleasant to spend the afternoon with a good book. Cristy lay on her stomach on the cool grass, reading. Abby, soft and furry, lay within the crook of her arm. While Charles and Cristy had been adventuring, Mr. Todd had set up a ladder against Abby's refuge. With a long pole he had poked her within reaching distance and brought her to earth. Now she purred contentedly. Robins sang from the cherry orchard. Tomboy was interested only in slumber. The Todds napped within the house.

"Boy, this is the best book!" Cristy squirmed with pleasure. "But no wonder! Didn't I choose it from the library shelf because it's by my favorite author, Deborah Bruce?" Cristy read on.

"Did you see the mailman, Cristy?" called Mrs. Todd.

Cristy tried to wrench herself from the world which Deborah Bruce had unrolled between book covers. "I haven't noticed," answered Cristy, only half hearing a voice, only half seeing a shape dressed in Mrs. Todd's clothes.

"I'm expecting a letter from the city." Mrs. Todd tripped out to the mailbox and back again. "Nothing but an advertisement and the July number of *The Hog World* for George," she announced.

"Ummmmm," murmured Cristy. As the cat stole away, it was no more to her than a small shadow on the grass. She did not see Mr. Todd leave the house. She did not notice Tomboy get up, turn around twice, and resettle himself. She read on, laughing and crying. She was so eager that she skipped a little. But she was naturally a fast reader. She came to the final paragraph. "Brother!" Rejoicing, Cristy rolled over on her back. "Ouch!" It was those scratches again.

Cristy ran into the house. She thrust her book under Eva Todd's nose. "This is the most outstandingest book I ever read in my whole life!" she cried.

"When my Mary was about your age," observed Mrs. Todd, smiling, "she wrote to an author whose books she liked. I can't even remember the author's name. But she answered. You can

imagine how thrilled Mary felt! I suppose she still has that letter tucked among her keepsakes."

Cristy sank into a chair, stunned at the thought of anyone writing to an author. Surely no one on Finney Street had ever thought of it. Momma would be horrified at such unheard-of boldness.

But Mrs. Todd seemed amazingly different.

"I would be scared to do it!" exclaimed Cristy, breathlessly. "I wouldn't have the nerve! I don't know where she lives. Do you suppose she'd really answer?"

"Even if she doesn't answer, you would have the pleasure of sending her your compliments. You will find a tablet and ball pen in the desk. Address your letter in care of the publishers. We can mail it in Hicksburg this evening."

Cristy sat motionless. Only her eyes danced. Should she? Shouldn't she? "What shall I write?" she whispered.

"In a letter of that kind, you should write what you feel. A booklover like you should be able to write what is in your mind and heart."

Cristy crept to the desk. She sat down, pen in hand, the fair white sheet spread before her. What was in her mind and heart? At this critical moment, *nothing.* Help!

Cristy held inward talk with herself. The neighborhood library on Finney Street—had it not been her joy and salvation? Mrs. Rozell, always eager to share with Cristy a book which she herself had enjoyed. Cristy's own name on the big poster, the name of a girl who loved to read more than anything. Ten shining paper stars, won by the end of summer. Reading aloud to Momma and little Carlotta, the words hanging themselves up in memory, like the everlasting stars of the sky.

But as so often happens with other hopeful letter writers, clear meanings and words of beauty remained somewhere beyond Cristy Romano. She wrote:

> Dear Deborah Bruce:
> I am visiting in the country. But in the city where I live, I am in Summer Reading Adventure at the library. I have read most of your books, and I like them the best. I suppose you are far off, but while I am reading your stories I feel that you are my close friend. They give me a very nice feeling inside. This morning I rode a horse. I wish you would write a horse story. I would read it. But I think books are wonderful no matter what they are about. I am going back to my home on the third of July. If you could answer this, I would like it very much. But if you don't want to, don't. Whatever happens, it has been a thrill writing to you.
> Your Loving Reader, Cristina Romano

Mrs. Todd read the letter. She said it was nice. She advised Cristy to copy it on a fresh sheet. "I will give you two postage stamps," said Mrs. Eva. "One is to pay the United States for carrying your letter. One is for Miss Bruce to send an answer, in case she does."

Cristy could easily have drowned in her bath that afternoon, so dazed was she at having written to an author. She scarcely knew what food she put in her mouth at supper. In the car, she held her letter by the merest finger tip, fearing she might get a tiny smudge on it. In Hicksburg, she walked stiff-legged into the little post office, and dropped the letter into the slot. Oh, happy day! Oh, living hope!

10. "WONDERFUL"

IS THE WORD

ONE morning Cristy and Charles again took the back road to play with Susan and Ann. In the barn loft they were trapeze performers. They leaped through space. They swung through air. They whirled and tobogganed and somersaulted. It was all a little dangerous. Cristy hadn't known she could be so daring—a girl who had lain trembling in her bed that first night in the country, for fear of falling stars.

At mid-morning the children enjoyed a snack under the trees on the lawn. As they ate, they joked about the playful bough which had swept Cristy off the horse. Now they couldn't even tell which one it had been.

"I want to take Cristy for a boat ride," suggested Ann. How she loved the pond!

Cristy was eager. The four children ran to the pasture, in whose center the pond lay like a round blue eye. Four cows stood at one edge, in reedy shallows. Susan picked up a stick. Without the least fear, she drove the cows to a clump of trees in the distance.

The children paddled around in the boat. Cristy could not have been more wonder-struck had she found herself a passenger on an Atlantic liner.

"Cristy and I like this," Ann protested when Susan and Charles

grumbled that it was hot and glaring on the water. "Surely you want to fish!" cried Ann.

"Not me!" Charles refused. He was pleased when Susan suggested a game of ping-pong in the cool basement of the Reed farmhouse.

"You two go ahead, then. Don't mind us," called Ann. She had worked up a fierce ardor for the sport of fishing. She kept a can of angle worms in a bed of ferns in one of the pasture fence corners. Now she grounded the boat and ran for the worms. She baited lines for herself and Cristy. She showed how a good fisher girl trails her line while the boat drifts slowly over the water.

"It's all so different from Finney Street," mused Cristy. "I wish Nick were here. I wish Wiggsy and Miss Pat could see us. If only Marie Azarello could lay eyes on us, and So-She-Ate-Cherries and Mrs. Rozell the librarian." Which inspired Cristy to confide that she had written to an author. "I sent her a postage stamp," Cristy revealed.

Ann almost overturned the boat. "If you aren't crazy!" she cried. "You're always *going* for something! But hush up, now. We don't want the fish to know we're here. I'll feel sunk if we don't catch any."

The slow sunny moments dreamed over the quiet water, over the quiet pasture and the cattle lying quietly under the trees. Ann let out a little scream when she caught a four-inch fish. Cristy yelled faintly when she caught one about the same size. She shouted when she hooked a second one a fraction larger.

"You're just a natural with a fishing pole," Ann complimented Cristy. When a summons was heard from the house, Miss O'Bannon added, "I'll give you my fish, so that you will have three."

Cristy was proud to carry the morning's catch to the Todds. "There's one for each of us," she boasted. The little fish were scarcely worth cleaning. But Mrs. Todd did it. She rolled them in corn meal and fried them in a tiny pan. They shrank. On the three dinner plates they appeared as the merest snippets. Cristy deigned to eat a slice of the pot roast which had been simmering all morning. But oh, the extraordinary fish she had contributed to the noonday meal! Mr. Todd, noting how glory-smitten she seemed, speared his fish, put it into his mouth, with room to spare, and rhymed:

> "This fish is fit for the gods,
> As well as for the Todds."

He went on to say that the robins were about to take all the cherries. "We had better start picking this afternoon. Cristy, you may help if you like."

"I'd love to," agreed Cristy. She had seen the ripe cherries hanging in the trees like giant candies. "Cherries," she pondered, "that's the name of the lady who bought my clothes and paid my bus fare out here—So-She-Ate-Cherries."

"I'll bet!" Mr. Todd joked airily, and Mrs. Todd added, "You don't say!"

"It's true! There's a lady's picture hanging in the lower hall at Dexter House. I think it must be her."

"I'll bet!" said Mr. Todd again, and went out to see if the mailman had left anything as interesting as *The Hog World*.

"I hope you bring back the letter I'm dying for," Mrs. Todd called after him.

"This is it, Eva," announced Mr. Todd, when he returned. He waited for her to open and read the letter. He watched as she began to smile and then to laugh. "Goody!" cried Mrs. Eva, as if she were a delighted child. "George, they're coming!" She handed the letter to him.

Mr. Todd chuckled as he read the letter. "Shall we tell Cristy now?" he asked.

"This minute!" exclaimed Mrs. Todd. "Cristy, the letter is from your brother Nick."

"My brother Nick Romano?" echoed Cristy. "I didn't know he ever wrote letters. Whatever—"

"Remember the day I told you to run away while I had a private talk with your mother?" Mrs. Todd reminded Cristy. "It was then I invited her to come to our farm while you are here, and bring the other children. I want to meet your mother. I want her to enjoy a vacation from the city heat."

Mr. Todd was nearest Cristy's flinging arms. "Oh, Daddy George!" she caroled. "Oh, Mrs. Eva, I don't know what to say! But it is the *most!*" Cristy hurled herself so violently upon her hostess that the dining table rocked.

"Your family is to come on the Friday of your last week end with us—that's next Friday—and on the following Tuesday you will all go back on the bus which is to pick up the children who are vacationing in Caspar County."

Cristy counted on her fingers. How many days until then? How many days and nights for Momma and the others to stay?

"So your mother said she would talk it over with your father, and let me know. Aren't you going to read Nick's letter?"

"Dear Sir and Mrs," Nick had written.

"Mrs. Romano says to thank you with all her hart and okay she will come and bring us. Pop hass to work on Sattadays. He won't be coming but thanks ennyway. At first I said nothing doing I cant leave my bizness. But I can. Its your horse. So long until Friday on the bus you said to take. Sincerly. Nick Romano."

At any other time, Nick's spelling would have distressed Cristy. But what matter "hart" and "ennyway" and "bizness" when one's brother was so dear as to write for Momma? What difference about "Sattaday" and "sincerly" when every word made a sister so blazing happy?

"Could I telephone Ann?" begged Cristy.

"Of course," answered Mr. Todd, who had now quite easily become Daddy George. "You might also ask Ann if she and Susan would enjoy picking cherries with us. Tell her they may eat all the cherries they want, within reason."

Over the telephone Cristy pealed her message to Ann. "Guess what a scrumptious thing is going to happen! My folks are coming, my momma and Nick and Carlotta and little Dory! Everybody except Poppa. They will sleep and eat and visit here. I don't see how I can wait until Friday."

The right kind of squeals were coming from Ann. When Cristy had heard enough of them to feel completely satisfied, she caroled good-bye. She then remembered about the cherry picking. She had to call Ann again, waiting while it was talked over with Susan. "We'll be right over," promised Ann. "I never did have all the cherries I want."

"Listen, Ann," prattled Cristy. "I forgot to tell you that it isn't So-She-Ate-Cherries who's paying to get my folks out here. Mrs. Eva and Daddy George—that's what I'm calling them now—well, they *invited* my folks! It's the wonderful Todds doing the whole wonderful thing. Isn't that wonderful?"

Cristy hung up, feeling so absolutely *wonderful* that during the dish wiping she flapped her dishtowel wildly and broke a saucer. She was stunned with remorse. Mrs. Eva only laughed. "The dish is so cracked as not to be sanitary. I'm glad I shall never have to see it again," she declared.

"That's wonderful," Cristy gushed. "You are wonderful. Everything is wonderful."

Cristy never did remember much about the cherry picking that afternoon. It was little more than a dream—in her fingers the clusters of scarlet fruit; in the pail the growing mound of treasure; in her mouth the roundness and juiciness of cherry after cherry; in her ears the lively chatter of Charles, Susan and Ann, perched like robins in the neighboring trees. The real thing was Nick's letter on the table in the farmhouse. The real thing was Momma in Number Fifty-One, getting ready to come to Caspar County. Or could it be real? Was it also but a dream?

"Are you too mad to talk to us, Cristy?" called Ann.

Cristy came to, for a moment. "Mad?" she asked in surprise. "No. It's wonderful!"

"Wonderful, wonderful!" mocked Ann, laughing. "Can't you think of any word but 'wonderful'?"

11. THE ROMANOS ARRIVE

"*I*T'S day after tomorrow they come, isn't it? We shall be busy getting ready for them, won't we?" There was no mistaking what Cristy meant by *it* and *them*.

Getting ready for the Romanos! Cristy spun about like a whirlwind. She gathered eggs, feeling that she should make a bow and thank each laying biddy. She peeled summer apples and rhubarb. She stemmed cherries and shelled peas. She lingered in the kitchen, inhaling deep, blissful whiffs of oven fragrance— Mrs. Eva's wonderful breads, pies, and cookies. Vegetables and meats and fruits were cooked and sealed for deep freezing.

Cristy was so excited that Daddy George almost had to coax her for a riding lesson. After all her earlier plans she could scarcely put her mind to it. Yet she grew more and more interested. It became thrilling to move slowly around the pasture alone, high and proud in the saddle. Daddy George sat on the fence, watching closely, and calling quiet directions to her. Quietly also he talked to the horse, who was so understanding and obedient, and knew so much more about the whole thing than Cristy. If ever there was a gentleman, it was Old-Timer. Daddy George said that Cristy was not ready to ride for prizes. But he praised her. She herself felt a new bond with the boys and girls in books who love and ride horses.

By Friday morning Cristy's joy was so great that everything around her, even Tomboy, seemed to glitter. Now she filled the house with vases of fresh flowers. She helped Mrs. Eva prepare the beds. Momma would sleep with Cristy in the double bed in which a certain city child had huddled and wept her first night. "Wasn't it wacky?" Cristy laughed at herself as she patted the nest made for baby Salvadore in a big clothesbasket. How thrilled Nick would be to sleep on a cot on the upper porch! Carlotta was to have a pretty little spool bed by the side of the Todds' big one.

"By-the-way," asked Mrs. Eva, "does Carlotta look like you?"

"Not much," answered Cristy. "Carlotta is pretty."

After a hurried noonday snack, Daddy George made ready to start for the county seat to meet the bus. He suggested that Cristy remain at home. "I think it would be nice for your mother to see you first at the farmhouse," he said. "Somehow it sets the stage."

The hour of waiting seemed much longer than sixty minutes. But at last the car turned into the driveway. Momma was getting out, her arms so full of fat Dory and she herself so plump that she could scarcely squeeze through the door. She exchanged greetings with Mrs. Eva. She kissed Cristy. She stood still, lifting her face to country sunshine and wind, to country beauty and peace.

And there was Carlotta, shy and smiling, showing the gap where her tooth used to be. There was Nick, looking so intently for Old-Timer that he might as well have shouted, "Quick, where's that horse I came to see?"

"Over there in the pasture, Nick!" Cristy pointed. "His name is Old-Timer. And see that house?" Cristy turned Nick around. "That's where Charles lives. Charles wants to take you exploring along the river."

Nick glanced at Charles's house. He turned and took a long

look at Old-Timer. A real horse! Suddenly Nick was down with Tomboy in a joyous tumble of shouts and barks, kicking boy-legs and wagging dog-tail, flailing boy-arms and licking dog-tongue.

Dory fought off Cristy's kisses with his chubby fists. But she gave him another smothering embrace before inviting Nick and Carlotta to see the farm. "Come on," she urged. As she led them away, she kept up a steady stream of eager talk.

"Now here's the chicken house. Hens lay eggs every day, for free. Here is the barn, like in storybooks. I'll show you where things grow right up out of the ground and don't cost a single cent. There are flowers. Not in a shop behind glass, either. Over there in the field are hogs for bacon. In the pasture our cows eat grass and give milk we don't have to pay for."

"I want to go and see the horse right now," Nick demanded. "I want to climb on the fence and maybe touch his nose."

Brother and sister began streaking toward the pasture. But

Lotta settled herself in the barn doorway, with Abby curled in her lap. What small six-year-old would wish to try to keep up with the leaping feet of Nick and Cristy, when she could sit quietly in the sun and cuddle a dear little cat?

Cristina looked back at Carlotta. Her gaze traveled on to the farmhouse. Momma was sitting on the side porch, rocking Dory. She had her shoes off. She and Mrs. Eva were talking at a great rate. How comfortable! How friendly! As Cristy turned again to catch up with Nick, her heart was a bubble of lightness. Her folks, her beloved Romanos, invited, arrived, and happy!

This same wonderful "togetherness" was felt by everyone around the supper table. The last delicious bite was scarcely taken when Charles arrived.

He led Nick away to explain the farm machinery.

The Reeds came by car. Momma was pleased, but not very surprised, to see Ann O'Bannon. "Ann came on bus to Caspar County. She would be around," reasoned Momma.

The older children played hide-and-go-seek. They sought hiding places among the trees and bushes, in the barn and machinery sheds. They hid in the chicken house. The hens had gone to bed. They made fretful noises because their rest was disturbed. Carlotta went to sleep on Daddy George's lap. One glance at Daddy George, and everyone knew that he was bewitched by curly-haired Carlotta Romano.

It grew too dark to play outside. The stars came out. After plans were made for another picnic Sunday evening, the Reeds departed. Mrs. Westover telephoned. It was Charles's bedtime. Why didn't he come home? "Because Nick Romano is here," answered Charles, simply. But Mr. Todd was already marching Nick off to the shower in the basement. Charles was obliged to go home. Bedtime is something which arrives every night, sooner or later. Generally, sooner.

Mrs. Todd went to see that Carlotta was comfortable. On the dark porch Momma yawned. "Long, long day, Cristina. Eighty miles away is city. Wonder how is Poppa."

"You're not homesick, Momma?"

"No, no," chuckled Momma. "I feel fine. Cristina, now we look at stars together?" She heaved herself up out of her chair. In the yard she gazed up at the wide sky. She drew a happy sigh. "Like in Italy," breathed Momma. "Like long time ago." She drew Cristy closer. "Remember these stars, girl. Beautiful to remember."

12. A HORSE, A PETUNIA,
AND A PICNIC

NICK spent the next morning with Old-Timer. He didn't seem to care about riding. All he wanted was to stand and gaze. All he wanted was to stroke the satiny nose and pat the satiny neck. He had heard about grooming a horse. "Could I do it?" he asked. Mr. Todd brought Old-Timer from the pasture into the barnyard. The boy was shown how to clean him with currycomb and brush. Old-Timer enjoyed it. Nick loved every minute of it. He loved every inch of the horse, including those inches he was not tall enough to reach.

"Don't you want to go exploring along the river, Nick?" fretted Charles Westover. "I know a place which is almost a cave. Don't you want to crawl into it and play 'lost'? Don't you want to swim in the river?"

"Maybe tomorrow," answered Nick.

"Tomorrow's Sunday."

"Monday, then."

"Monday is—well, it's Monday. It might rain or something," Charles argued. "What'd you come to the farm for, anyway?"

"To see a real horse," answered Nick. "To do what I'm a-doing now." Nick polished Old-Timer's rump. It is a part of a horse where polish shows to best advantage.

"Suit yourself." Charles walked away, head bent. On the farmhouse lawn he slumped down beside Cristy, playing there with Dory. "Combing and brushing all day, Nick could rub that horse raw," growled Charles.

Cristy informed the noonday dinner circle that Charles was disappointed because Nick wouldn't go on a river hike.

"Nick Romano, you play at river," scolded Momma. "It's nice invitation from Charles. You want to do only one thing on vacation, like combing a horse all the time?"

"Look at Cristy, Mom," begged Nick. "Cristy hasn't done a thing all day but play with Dory."

"But before Dory came I rode a horse," Cristy explained. "I rode in a boat. I caught fish. I looked at stars. I picked flowers and fed chickens and wiped dishes and read my books. I did 'most everything."

"Well, there's Carlotta!" cried Nick. "She's been squatting among the flowers all morning, like she was glued there! Lotta stares at flowers all the time. I curry a horse all the time. So what?"

"Too much currying could make Old-Timer sore, Nick," Daddy George spoke up. "You could make him so fond of you he might cry real tears when you go back to the city."

This compliment put Nick in such an amiable mood that he said good-bye to Old-Timer and trudged off to the river with Charles. They stayed and stayed. Supper had been over an hour and the grownups feeling anxious before they returned. The boys were tired and dirty, but glowing with adventures remembered.

"What did you do?" inquired Cristy.

"Nothin' much," they answered.

But now that he was back from a most glorious afternoon, and had eaten a good supper, Nick did not wish to waste another

minute away from Old-Timer. Charles was obliged to spend the
evening seated with Nick on the edge of the horse's feedbox.
Merely by raising his hand in the darkness, Nick could stroke
Old-Timer's nose. "You're hipped on this horse," observed
Charles, jealously. His remark did not bother Nick in the least.
It was wholly true.

Daddy George took the others for a ride in the car. The dewy
fields on either side of the quiet country roads smelled sweet.
Cristy sat with the driver. She related a story to him. It was the
wonderful tale by Deborah Bruce which Cristy had recently read.
Daddy George listened with interest. Twice during the telling
he asked, "Could that have happened in real life, do you think?"

"It did happen, Daddy George. I've just told you!" cried
Cristy.

Carlotta sat in the back between Momma and Mrs. Eva. Scenery
without and chatter within, passed by, and over her. For Carlotta
had a secret. It lay in her warm little palm. Her fingers were
curled carefully around it. Carlotta didn't know it by name. She
didn't know that Mrs. Eva's seed catalog listed its variety as

"ruffled little giants pink frills." It was a pink petunia. It was
just one small but precious memento of Carlotta's enchanted day.
When she climbed into bed and relaxed in sleep, her fingers un-
curled. There lay the petunia, its frills crushed, but still faintly
fragrant.

On Sunday morning, Daddy George took Cristy and Nick and
their mother to church at the county seat. Carlotta woke late.
No sooner had she finished her breakfast than she skipped off
to the garden. It was just as if she were keeping a promise.
It was as if petunias and pansies, columbine and larkspur had

said to her yesterday, "Will you come back, little Carlotta?"— and she had answered, "Yes, I will come tomorrow."

Mrs. Eva fretted. "Carlotta will get a painful sunburn," she said, when her guests returned from church.

Momma turned a tender look on garden and child. "Flowers don't grow out of city sidewalks. . . . But, yes, Cristina, run and coax Carlotta into doing something different."

In the garden Cristy used words of persuasion. "Come, sister. See how poor Abby rubs herself against your legs, begging you to play."

Carlotta pointed to the throng of upturned pansy faces. "They talk to me," she declared, raising luminous eyes to Cristy. "All those pretty bugs talk to me." She pointed to the bees, buzzing over the blossoms.

Cristy picked up the cat, and placed her in Carlotta's arms. "Momma says to come," she said firmly. Carlotta trotted out of the garden with Cristy.

After dinner the Todds and their guests sat on the lawn. Only Carlotta, drugged with flower shapes and flower colors, and Dory, sleepy with babyhood, napped in the house. Presently a long sleek automobile passed on the highway.

"Brother, what a car!" murmured Nick, too full of Sunday food and strict orders from Momma to be brushing Old-Timer. Now the car came back. The young man driving turned it into the Todd driveway. Cristy took one astonished look at him, and at the bareheaded girl smiling beside him. Leaping to her feet, Cristy tore across the lawn. "Miss Pat!" she cried.

"It's Miss Logan from Dexter House!" exclaimed Nick. He and the Todds hastened to the car.

Miss Pat embraced Cristy. She shook hands with the Todds.

She explained her arrival. "This is my friend, Ken Russell. We like this part of the state. On Saturdays or Sundays we sometimes drive up here. Knowing that Cristy Romano was staying with a couple named Todd, and remembering the rural route number, Ken and I thought it would be fun to look you up."

"Welcome." Mr. Todd's eyes twinkled as he took Miss Pat's hand. "When I saw such a gorgeous car turning in, and that our Cristy is acquainted with such a gorgeous young lady, I felt pretty sure you must be the great So-She-Ate-Cherries herself."

Cristy heard. Her breath seemed to stop. Her startled glance flew to Daddy George's face, and then to Miss Pat. Yes, Pat Logan was gorgeous in a truly elegant way. She wore clothes which only a person as rich as So-She-Ate-Cherries could afford. Cristy stared and blinked and stared again, as if she were half blinded by a dazzling beam of light.

Miss Pat bent to her. "You're just bowled over with the surprise of seeing me, aren't you?" She laughed. "Sugar, you're brown. You've gained weight. You're twice as pretty."

Mrs. Eva told the new arrivals about the river picnic planned for evening. "We'd be happy to have you join us," she said.

Ken said that it would be a long drive back to the city, and traffic would be heavy. "But I never could resist a picnic," he added. Miss Pat said she wanted to see Ann O'Bannon. They would stay.

The picnic was perfect, and everyone merry. After the meal, Cristy and Ann enjoyed a little stroll along the river with Miss Pat. "There's something I'd like to ask," ventured Cristy. "What is the name of the lady whose picture hangs in the main hall of Dexter House?"

"I thought all the children knew that," answered Miss Pat.

"The lady and the man whose portraits hang there, are the Dexters. They are no longer living. But thirty years ago they had the settlement house built. They paid for it. They left money to keep it going. Dexter House was named for them."

"Oh," said Cristy. The light within her grew.

"Oh," Ann remarked, and tossed a careless pebble into the water.

When good-byes were said, Cristy slipped eager arms around Miss Pat's waist. "Thank you," Cristy whispered. "Thank you for everything."

Miss Pat ruffled Cristy's hair. "There's nothing you need to thank me for, chum."

"But all the same, Miss," Momma called out, "thank you for your kindness to my Cristina."

Then Momma also knew that So-She-Ate-Cherries was really Miss Pat Logan! But if it were such a secret that no one talked about it, Cristy herself would keep quiet.

13. GOOD-BYE
TO OLD-TIMER

*I*T was Tuesday, the final morning of the Romanos' visit on the Todd farm.

"I'm going to ask." Cristy overheard Mrs. Eva's whisper.

"Want me to do it?" offered Daddy George.

"Please." Mrs. Eva seemed flushed and excited.

Long before it was necessary, Momma was ready to leave. She sat in a chair, gloved and hatted. Somehow she looked *gone*. Gone from the Todd farm, gone from Caspar County. Something about Momma this morning made one see and feel Finney Street. Cristy was ready, in her good dress. Dory was ready for anything. Outside, on the step, Carlotta cuddled Abby. She had spoken her farewells to the garden and its froth of flowers.

"Cristina," Momma worried, "call your brother. He will get his clean shirt dirty."

"Wait, Cristy," said Daddy George. "Let Nick have a few more minutes to say good-bye to Old-Timer. . . . Mrs. Romano, my wife and I want you and Cristy to hear what we ask of you."

"Ask," said Momma. "We give if we can."

"It's Carlotta," began the farmer. "She has stolen our hearts. We'd like to keep her for a while."

"For the remainder of the summer, Mrs. Romano," begged Mrs. Eva. "Until school begins."

Momma stopped rocking. "School, yes, Carlotta will be in

first grade." Momma removed her gloves. She drew her clean handkerchief from her purse and wiped her moist hands. "A minute please, for surprise to cool off?" she asked. "I will study for a minute about Poppa. I will study what Poppa will think."

Everyone waited for Momma to study.

"It would be good for Carlotta to stay," she said, at last. "On Finney Street Carlotta plays on dirty sidewalk. . . . Cristina, listen how kind of our friends to invite Carlotta. Cristina, what do you think?"

"It would be lonesome at home without Carlotta." A sudden lump filled Cristy's throat.

"When you say 'lonesome' you are thinking of Cristina Maddalena Romano," declared Momma, sternly. "Think for Carlotta."

"She might be homesick," offered Cristy, remembering.

"Mrs. Todd and Mr. Todd, excuse." Momma left her chair. "Cristina and I will explain to Carlotta."

On the porch Cristy listened while Momma sat and explained. "Farm is nice. Mr. and Mrs. Todd love you. The rest of the summer, my Carlotta, without your momma and poppa, without your sister and brothers."

Carlotta's big dark eyes were round with thought. "But after summer, I would come home and go to school?"

"In plenty time for school."

Carlotta climbed into her mother's lap. Her arms went around her mother's neck. "Sometimes I would love you too much. Sometimes I might want to see you," she said. "But I like the little bed I sleep in. I like the cat." Carlotta turned and looked across to the garden. "The flowers," she whispered, "I like the flowers very much. Momma, I will stay."

The busload of children returning to the city was more quiet than the one which had come to Caspar County two weeks before. There was that sober, let-down feeling which vacationers have when their holidays are over. Before Cristy had the coveted chance, Nick slipped into the same seat with Momma and the sleeping Dory. Just sitting there beside Momma, so large, familiar and steady, was comforting to Nick. He sat silent, but his thoughts were like words. "Old-Timer is the greatest."

He remembered how he had trudged out to Old-Timer's pasture to say good-bye. In his pocket was a carrot. In his hand was the

grooming brush. "Just a few last strokes," said Nick to himself. He climbed over the gate to the pasture side. It was easier than the chore of unlatching and latching again. Old-Timer came trotting, his ears pointed with question. He bent his head to nuzzle Nick's ear. It was a tickle so gossamer and velvety that it made Nick laugh in delight.

"You know me! You like me!" Nick cupped the horse's muzzle in his palm. "But fella, we've got to bear it. I s'pect we'll never see each other again."

And thinking of the myriad turning of wheels on the flinty pavements of Finney Street, and the tall, dingy buildings crowding his part of a city where horses are few and green pastures are none, Nick added, "I'll prob'ly never even touch a horse again. I'll prob'ly never be palsy-walsy with a horse. Not ever!" For a moment Nick was overcome. He pressed his forehead against Old-Timer's cheek. "Anyway," sobbed Nick, "it wasn't any use bringing the brush. There isn't time. I've got to go. Here, fella, eat this carrot. You old fella. You—old—b-b-boy."

Forgetting the brush in his hand, Nick used his bare forearm to wipe the stain of boyish tears from Old-Timer's cheek.

Cristy met Nick plodding toward the barn as she ran to call him. When she saw his telltale eyes, she ran past him without saying anything. At the pasture gate she, too, reached out a hand to Old-Timer. She loved him, but only with gladness that for a little while she had known a horse. Any other animal as noble would have done. It was different with Nick. He had known his time was too short to learn to ride. He didn't care. His love for Old-Timer was all eager service, just being near, not talking about it, as Cristy would do on Finney Street. Nick loved the horse because he was Old-Timer, and none other.

On the bus Cristy sat with Ann O'Bannon. She had felt regret in looking her last on the farmhouse, the slat hammock, the gardens, the barn, the cat, the chickens, Charles, Old-Timer and Tomboy. At the station Cristy had wished she did not have to say good-bye to Daddy George and Mrs. Eva. If she had not been careful she could have cried as she kissed Carlotta. Yet she was glad for the small sister. Mrs. Eva had pointed to a store across from the bus station. "After you leave," Mrs. Eva told Cristy, "I'm going over there and buy Carlotta a ruffled pink pinafore. The night I found a pink frilled petunia in her hand as she lay sleeping, I thought how sweet she would look in frills."

So the good-byes had been said. Cristy's visit to the country was over. But her plans for the remainder of summer were as bright and hopeful as before. What a lot of talk she and Momma would pour out for dear Poppa! Tomorrow Cristy would return her books to the library, report on them, and see two stars added to her name. On the twenty-third of July the course in Baby Care would begin at Dexter House. Bruno would be coming home to Number Fifty-One in his sailor suit.

14. CRISTY

MAKES HER PLEA

*T*HE twenty-third of July fell on Monday. It was the day for Cristy's first lesson in Baby Care. By mid-morning she was skipping out of Angel Flats. She felt as hopeful and high-hearted as ever in her life. For a girl who loved babies, and particularly one baby—for a girl who had made a treasured wish on a star—the course in Baby Care should be wonderful.

When Cristy arrived at Dexter House and was directed to the proper room by Miss Pat, she was glad to see that it was Nurse Downing who was to teach the junior girls. The nurse was on regular duty at Dexter. Cristy was used to seeing her flitting starchily in and out of the day nursery, and through other parts of the building as she was needed.

Now she stood before the ten bouncy pupils. They were highly interested in her and in one another. But the object which drew most of their attention was the big baby doll lying on the enamel-topped table. At once Cristy began to feel a merry affection for the doll. It wore shirt, diaper, socks and dress. It had rosy cheeks, dimples, a painted blond curl on its forehead, and a delightful painted smile. Just now its feet were in the air, as if it might start kicking, or even sucking its toe. Beginning in a jolly way, Nurse Downing punched Baby Doll in its rubbery stomach. It gave a lifelike wail. "Who wouldn't?" joked Miss Downing. The girls jumped with mirth.

The nurse went on, seriously. "A human baby is the most helpless of all infant creatures. He remains helpless for a longer
period than animal babies do. As each child is born into a family,
it needs the most wise and tender care. The purpose of this new
course at Dexter House is to teach you big sisters the correct
sanitary routines. Our hope is that you will take into your homes
what you learn. We hope that you will realize that you are
partly responsible for your little brother or sister. You are old
enough to know that correct methods of bathing and feeding and
clothing are not enough, alone, to make a baby happy. To be
altogether contented and healthy, a baby must be loved."

For a moment Nurse Downing forgot what she had planned to say next, because of Cristina Romano. Shining dark eyes, flushed cheeks, parted smiling lips, that was Cristina.

Contented, healthy, loved! "It's Dory the nurse is talking about, and yet she's never seen him," thought Cristy.

"We shall now pretend that it is Baby's bath time," said Nurse Downing. "See how I place soap and oil and powder and towels and clean clothing ready at hand. Now here is how I prepare the bath. I test the water to make sure it is neither too hot nor too cold." Nurse went on, making little jokes to keep the girls laughing and interested. And when at last Baby Doll had been re-dressed, bottle-fed, and put to sleep, Miss Downing said that after today the girls would take turns going through the same routine.

"But things will come up," she warned. "Baby may suffer colic. He might push cotton up his nose. He might eat soap. He might stick a safety pin down his throat. He might tumble and bump his head. We must know what to do." The girls giggled, which perhaps reminded Miss Downing to remark that the junior class was small compared to the class of older girls being taught by a nurse from the baby hospital. "But because we are few," Miss Downing said, "we shall learn the faster, perhaps. Beginning with our fourth lesson, a real baby from the day nursery will model for us. Then you may show what you have learned from practising on the doll. The final and eighth lesson will be an oral quiz, without either doll or baby. To those who deserve it, I shall present a diploma bearing a gold seal in the shape of a star."

. . . Star bright,
. . . Wish I might.

The Monday and Thursday lessons became to Cristy a hope and a delight which she often whispered into the ear of Master Salvadore. She chattered about them at home until Momma said she didn't know why her children set their hearts so strongly on things—Cristina on Baby Care, the Summer Reading Adventure and the stars that went with them; Nick on the horse at the Todd farm; Carlotta on the flowers in the Todd garden.

Poppa had turned white when he saw his family return without Carlotta. But as soon as he learned that nothing had happened to her, he said she was better off in the country. When George Todd's postal card arrived, Poppa said that the farmer must be a guy with a good sense of humor. Cristy read the postal aloud to the family.

"My wife Eva is so busy playing with Carlotta that I must do the writing. All I'm doing just now, *ha, ha,* is to harvest fifty acres of wheat! Carlotta is as good as gold, happy as a lark, busy as a bee, and brown as a muffin just out of the oven. She is proud to be able to name the garden flowers correctly. But she has become interested in other things, Abby's family of four new kittens, for instance. She talks of all of you, but has not been homesick. Old-Timer moped for Nick for several days. We miss Cristy, and hope her summer ventures will turn out well. Thanks again for Carlotta."

Old-Timer had missed him! Nick was struck dumb with pleasure. But later he told his employer about it over the lettuces, watermelons and late strawberries at the fruit-and-vegetable stand. "One of these days," prophesied Mr. Ciello, "there won't be any such animal as a horse."

Mr. Todd's mention of her summer adventures made Cristy feel that she should apologize to Mrs. Rozell, the librarian. "I'm so busy," she explained. "But after my work in Baby Care is over, I can read faster and more."

"Skimming through a good book at top speed is bad," chided Mrs. Rozell. "Take it easy, Cristy. You still have time to enjoy the Summer Reading Adventure. Since yesterday I've been saving a new book for you."

When Cristy saw the name on the cover she was thrilled. She pointed to it. "I wrote to this author while I was in the country."

The eyes and mouth of Mrs. Rozell widened. "You wrote to Deborah Bruce? Have you had an answer?"

"No," admitted Cristy. Bravely she quoted Mrs. Eva. "But I had the pleasure of sending her my compliments."

Between Baby Care classes, Cristy read the new book. It gave her those "nice inside feelings." She felt so inspired by them that she hinted to Momma how she might write again to Deborah Bruce. Just a very small letter, asking, ever so briefly, "Remember me?"

"Cristina Maddalena Romano!" cried Momma, thoroughly shocked. "Is it manners I've taught you, or not? How can a lady write books with busybodies bothering her? Now forget it. Cristina, what day-nursery bambinos you working on now?"

"We begin on a real baby the next lesson," answered Cristy, joyously. "Momma, the girl who owned the big doll has left Baby Care class. She's not coming back, nor her doll, either. All she cared about was showing off her nice doll. Just imagine anyone dropping out of Baby Care!"

The nine girls who remained faithful pupils were all a-twitter when Nurse Downing appeared at the fourth lesson with a girl baby from the day nursery. She was like a pale, delicate flower, and Cristy's heart melted. Yet with inward gloating she knew that Master Salvadore Romano would make two of the flower baby. In the final grooming Nurse Downing brushed the infant's scant topknot over her finger and formed a silky roll that was both absurd and becoming. "A new hair-do for Miss Glamour Puss," joked the nurse. With the other girls, Cristy squealed in merriment. Yet again, she couldn't help comparing the one wispy curl with Dory's thick, healthy mass of glossy ringlets.

When the nurse dismissed the class, she asked Ann O'Bannon to return the baby to the nursery, as there were lesson materials to clear up. Cristy lingered, fidgety and wistful.

"What's on your mind, Cristina, that you do not go home?" inquired Miss Downing.

Cristy's answer spilled out in a breathless rush of words. "Please, Nurse, could my baby brother be the model once? Just once? He's so good and jolly. I could bring him myself."

Nurse was astonished. "It's been said all the time, Cristy, that we would use a baby from the day nursery. It's simple. It's safe. It's fair. Cristy, if you were allowed to bring your baby, then Marie and Ann and the others might clamor to bring their babies. How should we get around that?"

Cristy's face fell. She knew that fair play is highly thought of by the right sort of people. She herself believed in it. But now it was different. "Suppose we could think of some way to get around it?" she begged.

"We couldn't." Miss Downing's answer was as flat as a dime. She studied her enrollment list. "I see, Cristy, that you live in Angel Flats. To reach Dexter House you must cross four street intersections. Not one of them has a traffic cop. You and the baby in all that tangle!"

"I'm used to it. I do it all the time. I would die before I'd

let anything happen to Dory! Oh, please, Miss Downing—Marie
and Ann and Bertha don't care as much as I do!"

"How do you know?" Nurse behaved as if she thought Cristy
was giving herself airs.

"I know! Oh, I do know!"

Nurse let this claim pass as worthless. "By-the-way," she
asked, "how many floors up in Number Fifty-One?"

Cristy hated to tell. "Four," she murmured.

"That settles everything! Heavens! An eleven-year-old girl
carrying a heavy baby down four flights, and up again!"

Cristy dropped into a chair, too dreadfully disappointed to
stand. "All summer I've planned it," she said. "I wished on a
star. Over my left shoulder, Nurse! And I've promised my baby
brother a dozen times. The way he laughs and waves his arms
I'm sure he understands. He wants to come. Oh, Miss Downing,
it isn't the diploma and the big gold star I care so much about!
It's giving Dory a treat."

"And perhaps showing him off?" suggested Miss Downing.

"But he's so beautiful! Everyone would enjoy him. You would
love him. Honest!"

Miss Downing took Cristy's hand. "I'm sorry you wished and
dreamed of a plan that cannot be carried out. It's irregular in
every way. Wiggsy would say 'no' as quick as scat. You must
understand, Cristy, and give up the idea without any fuss."

Creeping down the main hall, Cristy chanced to meet Miss Pat.

"Chum, whatever is the matter? You look done for!" Miss
Pat took Cristy's hand. "I'll walk a block with you, while you
tell me your troubles."

Walking with Miss Pat, Cristy explained everything. With
grim fairness she named the reasons why Dory could never act

as model in Baby Care, as definitely outlined by Nurse Downing. "I don't want to raise a fuss," Cristy entreated. "But how can a thing be wrong and not regular when it's right for Dory and regular for me?"

"There, you have me," Miss Pat admitted. "Golly!" she added, under her breath. She gave Cristy's hand three quick squeezes.

"You could help, Miss Pat." Cristy was timid, yet pleading. Everything was at stake. "I hate to ask you, after all you've done for me already. But if *you* would tell Wiggsy about Dory, she'd listen. If *you* would say to her, 'it would be nice,' Wiggsy would think so, too. If Nurse Downing knew who you really and truly are, she'd let *you* decide that my wish should come true."

"For Pete's sake, Cristy, what can you mean? Who am I?"

"Excuse me, Miss Pat. I know it's your very own secret that you are So-She-Ate-Cherries. But ever since you and your boy friend came to the farm that Sunday, and Daddy George said it right out, I've known it was you who sent me and the other kids to the country and paid for everything."

Miss Pat drew Cristy to the inner side of the walk. Very suddenly she sank down on a doorstep. She fumbled blindly for her handkerchief. She held it over her mouth. She closed her eyes and held her breath until she felt sure of herself. Again she fumbled in her purse. She drew forth a small notebook and pencil.

She scribbled: "Look, Cristy, this is how the two words are written which have sounded to you like *So-She-Ate-Cherries.*"

ASSOCIATED CHARITIES

Cristy was acquainted with *charity*. But she could not remember having met *charities*. Miss Pat explained. "Together, the words mean that several charitable associations have combined, in order to give more intelligent help to those they wish to—to be kind to. Wiggsy told you in the beginning, Cristy, that Associated Charities is a body, not one person. I thought you understood."

"My momma says about Mrs. Harlovich, 'She's a nice, friendly body,'" Cristy explained. "Momma says to me, 'Don't be a busybody.' So that's what I thought—*body*. Then it wasn't you who gave me the treat to the country, Miss Pat."

"Goodness no, chum!" Miss Pat got to her feet rather unsteadily. "I'm due back at Dexter. Cristy, don't build your hopes too high of Dory ever becoming the star model in Baby Care class. But I'll talk to Wiggsy. I'll do what I can."

"G'bye, then." Turning toward home, Muggsy's Grill, Chin Ying's laundry, the second-hand place, the drugstore—windows, doors, passing people—these were to Cristy little more than are the clouds which float past the wings of an airplane.

It was Ciello's fruit stand which suddenly became real, as Nick called out to Cristy. He liked for those who knew him to remember that he was in business. At this moment he was also eager to say aloud the thing that sang in his mind.

"Hi, Sis! Bruno comes today!"

"Bruno said anywhere from the fifth to the seventh of August," answered Cristy, absently.

"Well, this is the sixth. I bet he comes today." Nick grinned from ear to ear.

Cristy drifted on, and finally into Number Fifty-One.

Momma turned. She gave Cristy a long, keen look. She lowered the flame under the simmering pot on the stove. She sat down in her rocker. "You mixed up somehow, Cristina Maddalena?" she inquired. "Stars fall out of your sky? Want to tell Momma?"

Cristy was not ready to tell of her long-held hopes for Dory, nor the probable ruin of those hopes. She could not go a step farther with Momma until she had the backing of Wiggsy and Dexter House. But this was a good time to break the news to Momma that she and Cristy had been altogether wrong in believing that Miss Pat was really So-She-Ate-Cherries.

Momma listened, her brow puckered as she tried to turn into sense the odd notion that Cristy, and Cristy alone, had held all summer.

"You learn that Miss Logan ain't the great, giving lady called So-She-Ate-Cherries," said Momma, at last. "So what? She's like always your friend. Friend you love. Friend that loves you. Okay. That's settled. That's good.

"Now—*Charity*. Your momma knows first-hand. Listen, my Cristina.

"Charity is your poppa coming home from work. He says, 'Today, Momma, I give two dollars to 'Sociated Charities.' I answer, 'Okay, Poppa, we manage somehow. Some are in worse fix than we are.' Charity is kind people helping your momma when Bruno's own poppa died and Bruno so little. Charity is Cristina and Nick Romano dropping penny in box for kids who don't have as much as Cristina and Nick. Charity is people in all parts of city sending two dollars, ten dollars, hundred dollars to help people they never laid eyes on. One time, dollars for Cristina and Ann and busload to the country. All times for sick people to hospital. For clothes and food. For all kinds of giving, Dexter House and all. That's 'Sociated Charities. Greatest kind of love in the world, Cristina."

The outer door opened softly. It swung wide. A navy blue cap perched jauntily on a sleek head, peeking in. Bruno Torelli!

"Hiya, Mom!" Bruno swept Momma up in a great bear hug. Over her shoulder, and above her excited cries and laughter, Bruno beamed at Cristy. "Hi, Mosquito Boat!" he shouted. Fresh sea breezes seemed to sweep through Number Fifty-One.

15. STRAIGHT TALK

*F*OR the first time Nick regretted that he had to work three hours a day for Mr. Ciello. If he were only free to spend every waking moment with his half brother! Bruno, trim as a lifeboat, was leaving a daily backwash of delight as he cruised up and down Finney Street, St. James, the Avenue, byways, nooks and crannies of this end of town. Bruno had grown up here. He knew everyone except recent newcomers, and these did not remain strangers long.

"Hiya, Sailor!"

"I'm shipshape, Mr. Catalona. And you?"

"Hi, Bluejacket!"

"Thanks, Mr. Ciello. I'm riding the waves, and how!"

"Velly glad to see you, Bluno."

"Ahoy, Chin Ying! How's the soap holding out?"

At the busiest spots, Bruno was likely to cry "Gangway!" He would spread his hands as if to clear the sidewalk. Tilting his cap so that it hung absurdly on one ear, Bruno would caper so toe-tip dainty that he had everyone roaring and clapping. He would swagger off as bold as brass, but with an engaging wink and grin. When Nick could do so, he would follow Bruno, oozing pride. *Skipper*—that's what Bruno called Nick.

Sometimes Cristy went on these hail-the-conquering-hero cruises. "We'll tack around and sail in here," announced Bruno, one day. He steered Cristy into Dexter House, and barged into Wiggsy's private office. Cristy was filled with spine-chilling astonishment when Bruno encircled Wiggsy's waist with his brawny navy-blue arm, and planted a hearty kiss on her cheek. She turned pink. She laughed. She liked it. When Bruno told her he had a tooth-ache, she asked him sternly if he had been brushing his teeth regularly. And had he not talked with a Navy dentist?

Bruno said yes, he had been told his tooth was in a bad way, and should not be neglected another minute. "But I wouldn't let him touch it," declared Bruno. "I thought I'd wait until my home dentist could see it. He will prob'ly say my tooth is as sound as a dollar."

"I doubt it, Bruno Torelli. Go to the dentist at once."

"Aye, aye, sir." Bruno saluted Wiggsy.

Cristy studied her. If only Cristina Romano knew the art of charming Wiggsy as well as Bruno Torelli seemed to know it! Twice more would the junior girls practice on a baby. Dory? Maybe by the seventh lesson his chance would come. In legends and fairy tales, seven is a magical number. Things happen at the seventh time. Surely, by now, Wiggsy had been told of Cristy's dearest desire. Nurse Downing would have reported it in her line of duty. Miss Pat had promised help. Why didn't Wiggsy say something to Cristy this minute, while she laughed and chattered with Cristy's own half brother?

"We'll make headway to the dentist's, Mosquito Boat," said Bruno, swinging out of Dexter House. "If Doc should break the news to me that my tooth is no good, I might pile up on the rocks. I need you floating alongside."

Cristy enjoyed the elevator ride to the third floor, where the dentist had his office. In the waiting room, Bruno looked at comics without seeing them. Cristy wished for a library book.

But they had only a few minutes' wait. The dentist appeared

and said he would have time to examine the tooth. "Looks bad," he decided. He took an X-ray. "This is Friday," he said. "Come back Monday. By that time I can tell you what's what." He injected a pain killer in Bruno's gum. Bruno yelled. "What? A big strong United States Navy man like you?" exclaimed the dentist.

"'Looks bad,'" echoed Bruno, out on the street. "Could be my whole leave will be ruined." When things were really serious Bruno did not use ship language.

Throughout the week end he huddled in Number Fifty-One, as grumpy as only a healthy young man can be when driven to it. He even began growling about Carlotta. "That sweet little kid sister!" he moaned, holding his jaw. "For a year, through fair weather and foul, I've thought of her. But was she here when her only half brother came home? No! She was on a farm eighty land miles away. How's that for a sailor's welcome?"

Momma made a poultice. She held it to Bruno's throbbing jaw. She made delicious hot soups for him. She fed him Italian cheese custard. She murmured pet names. She told him that perhaps he could spend a day with Carlotta on the farm, or even go out there and bring her home just before school opened.

On Monday morning Bruno tottered hopelessly off to the dentist. Cristy trudged hopefully to Baby Care class.

The same delicate girl baby was the model. Cristy was assigned to powder and pin her up and roll the one silky curl. "See how handy and gentle Cristy is," said Nurse Downing to the class. At such lovely praise, Cristy came near dropping the little brush.

"Cristina Romano is wanted in Mrs. Wiggs's private office." It was Miss Pat's voice at the open door of the classroom.

Cristy's heart almost jumped out of her throat. Her eyes were large with questions as she walked through the hall with her friend. Miss Pat's tones were secret.

"Wiggsy, Nurse Downing and I went into a huddle. Or was it a tussle?" Miss Pat giggled. "Anyway, it went on for hours. Wiggsy is on the side of fair play and rules. She's definitely against showing favors to any one child. She's against giving in to a child's fantastic notions. The child—that's you, Cristy. The notions—that's your dream of Dory as a star performer in Baby Care. In a moment Wiggsy will be giving you some straight talk.

But whatever happens, Pal, remember that Wiggsy is pure gold. Whatever happens, keep your chin up."

In the office, Cristy was aware of Wiggsy's chin, as square as chins come. Wiggsy's crisp-as-celery voice seemed just off the ice.

"Cristina Romano, I would advise you not to do any more wishing on stars without first reasoning whether the wish is simply impossible of coming true. It is also bad if the wish is going to upset a large neighborhood settlement house and the people who are trying to run it sensibly and for the good of all."

"I only wanted—" (oh, something so simple!)

"Hush, Cristina. Let me advise that hereafter you pay attention to what is said to you at Dexter House. Surely you did not listen when I told you that Associated Charities is an organized body and not a person. Perhaps you would not understand why Pat Logan was so touched and upset when she learned from your own lips your belief that she was your fanciful So-She-Ate-Cherries, a great, bountiful person who sent thirty-five children, including you, to Caspar County. Where's your sense, Cristina? You read. You should have known the meaning of both words, 'associated,' and 'charities.' "

"I know them now," quavered Cristy. "*Then,* they sounded different. Miss Pat is so very good to me. Marie says she's rich. Daddy George said—oh, I would never mean to upset dear Miss Pat!" A sob, away down in Cristy's stomach, struggled to stay down. Her mouth trembled.

She was drawn within the circle of Wiggsy's arm. Now Wiggsy's voice was not so much like celery as cheese custard. "Nurse Downing reports that you are her best pupil. You pay remarkably close attention. You are naturally handy with babies, very gentle and understanding. Downing thinks you might become a baby-hospital nurse, some day."

"I love babies," sniffled Cristy.

"That's as plain as the nose on your face," Wiggsy agreed. "Now, Cristina, against my best judgment, I have been persuaded by some soft-hearted people around here to allow you to carry out this star-gazing wish of yours. That is, if we can climb over two big IF'S. Next Thursday, Nurse Downing will ask the other girls if they mind your bringing your brother to model for the seventh lesson."

"Seventh!" breathed Cristy. Trustfully she lifted her chin.

"If the girls say, 'Why is it fair for Cristy to do it more than us?'— Heavens, I can just hear them—promise me that you will accept their 'no,' and without feeling 'mad,' as you children say."

"I promise." Fair play—there is no getting around the fact that it is right, although sometimes hard to take.

"That's the first big IF, whether the girls will consent," Wiggsy went on. "The second big IF . . . By the way, Cristina, does your mother know of your plans for Salvadore?"

"Not yet," answered Cristy. "I knew you had to say 'yes' first."

"For once you used your head. Now, Cristina, in case you succeed in persuading your mother, then the second big IF is getting the baby here, safely. He must be brought by your mother, or some other strong, trustworthy person. If you clearly understand the IF'S, Cristina, you may go."

Cristy couldn't help a little skip as she started for the door. There she turned. "Please, Wiggsy, I would like to give you a compliment. Miss Pat says you are pure gold. I think so, too."

Hippity-hop went Cristy to the Angel Flats. But she neared them, slow stepping. With what glowing words could she make Momma understand that one big IF depended on her?

At first, in Number Fifty-One, Cristy could not even catch Momma's attention. Bruno had it all. Bruno had received shocking news at the dentist's office. He told it to Momma in detail, while Cristy and Nick listened.

"Doc said I'd waited too long, and my tooth's not worth trying to save," moaned Bruno. "Doc said, 'Come back tomorrow, Sailor, at ten ayem. I can give you gas, if you like.' But after a minute I told him I don't like to face danger with my eyes shut. 'It's up to you, Sailor,' said the doc. 'And never fear, I can yank that tooth out in a jiffy.'

"*Yank,*" muttered Bruno. "I don't like that word. It sounds mean."

As a United States bluejacket, Bruno had pledged his sacred honor that he would give his life for his country, if he had to. Often, on moonlight nights or when the band played, he had cherished visions of himself staying with his ship until the last wave washed over him. But having his tooth yanked out, that was an entirely different matter.

"Mom, if I could have some close relative with me tomorrow!" suggested Bruno, pitifully.

"My poor Bruno, your momma will go with you."

Bruno brightened, then shook his head. "Doc would think I'm 'chicken,' bringing my mother."

"Poppa, then?" asked Momma. "He might get off from work that long."

"Same thing. 'Chicken,'" decided Bruno.

"I'll go with you," Nick offered, eagerly.

"Good Skipper!" Bruno seemed relieved. But after deep study, he gave it up. "Little brother going with big brother. Doc would be dead sure I'm scared. But there's Cristy. She's a girl.

'Twouldn't enter Doc's head that a nineteen-year-old Navy man would bring his knee-high sister just because he had to have someone with him at yanking time. Some one loyal and true, Cristy. But look. If anyone asks, you're going with me tomorrow because you've never seen a tooth yanked out. See? It will be a new thrill for you. You're dying to go, see?"

"Ooo-ooh!" Cristy shuddered.

"Someone loyal and true, Cristina?" Momma was dazzled by the fine phrase. "Be a good girl and go with Bruno. You can bear it."

"I'll do it, Mom." And now, while Momma was in a tender mood, Cristy began, "Wiggsy says I can bring Dory to be the baby model for the seventh lesson, if—"

"What for?" inquired Momma, and Nick cried, "For Pete's sake, why?"

"A lovely treat for Dory, that's why!" cried Cristy. "Nurse makes such darling little jokes. We girls laugh. Everybody watches the baby, every minute. The bath and the nice soap and powder—it's all just wonderful. Dory will be the cutest ever. Nurse Downing will think so. Mom, there are two big IF'S." Cristy described them, while Momma tried hard to understand. She gave Cristy a straight look. "This summer all my children set their hearts on something. Bruno, you got your heart set on something?"

"My ship," answered Bruno.

Momma sighed with relief. "Okay," she said. She studied Dory, beating pans on the floor, "Another big If, Cristina," she declared. "What if something happen to Dory? His poppa wants the bambino to grow into another Mister Romano." Momma whirled on Cristy. "Did Wiggsy-lady invite Salvadore?

Or did you ask Wiggsy-lady?"

"I asked," Cristy admitted.

"Miss Bold-face!" accused Momma. "Writing letters to busy book authors! Making Wiggsy-lady trouble!"

"Oh, Mom, hold off," begged Bruno. "Don't you see that the little mosquito boat is about to pile up on the rocks? What's wrong with her, except she's got too much heart for her size? All heart, no mind, that's Mosquito Boat." Bruno's grin was too wide for comfort. "Ouch!" he yelped. His hand flew to his jaw.

Momma flared up. "How can you say your sister's got no mind? She's the best reader on Finney Street. Cristina, about carrying our Dory to Baby Care school—I'll talk it over with your poppa tonight."

16.   THE LAST BIG "IF"

NUMBER FIFTY-ONE was in a dither the
next morning. There was no thought for anyone but Bruno
Torelli, apprentice seaman. At nine-thirty, after bestowing fare-
well kisses on Momma and little Salvadore, he stumbled away
and up the street, seeing nothing. He held Cristy's hand in a tight
grip.

"One last thing, Cristy," he implored. "I may not be able
to speak when we reach Doc's office. So it's up to you to tell him
to be sure and save my tooth. I want to take it back to my ship
and show my buddies what I went through."

Cristy promised.

Arrived at the office, Bruno did not care for the dentist's greeting. It was too cheerful. Gingerly the sailor eased himself into
the chair. He was covered with snow-white cloths, given a large
mass of absorbent tissue, and tipped back at a frightful angle.
Before closing his eyes to shut out the view of all the various
rigging which was to dull the pain, loosen, and extract, Bruno
felt for Cristy. "You still here?" he whispered.

Cristy thought her heart would break. "Yes, dear half brother,"
she quavered. Her hand trembled over Bruno's left, as it gripped
the chair arm. She closed her eyes.

Therefore, neither the blind Cristy nor the blind Bruno saw
the steel grip the tooth. Thanks to the pain-killer, Bruno heard
the pull far more than he felt it. Cristy felt it keenly in her
imagination. But the yanking was a matter of seconds. "All

over!" pronounced the dentist. He was laughing, yet he was red
with embarrassment. "First time, in all my twenty years as a
dentist, that such a crazy thing has happened. I lost your tooth,
Sailor. It flew away from the forceps and right out of the window."

Bruno stared, his eyes glassy. Without a word, he heaved himself erect. He tossed aside all his white wrappings, except the
bib-towel around his neck. Holding tissue to his numb lips, he
grabbed Cristy's arm. Together they plunged out to the corridor,
popped into an elevator, and descended to street level. A moment later Bruno was earnestly stooping and creeping as he
searched sidewalk, gutter and street for the uprooted tooth which
had flown out of the window. Three stories above, the dentist

leaned out. "Bruno Torelli!" he shouted. "Get back up here and let me treat that hole in your jaw!"

Bruno paid no heed. The dentist gave up shouting. Neither did Bruno pay the least attention to the passers-by who bumped into and stumbled over him and Cristy. In a trice a curious crowd began to collect. Each person began to snoop and search. Some one—who was it?—had lost something of great value—but what? Perhaps it was a purse full of money, a gold watch, a lucky-number ticket, or even a parakeet.

"Hey, Cris, I see it!" Bruno's hands were suddenly firm under Cristy's armpits. He was lifting her. She reached. On the top of a parked car where it had fallen, Cristy laid fingers on the tooth. Above the bib around his neck, Bruno beamed as he and Cristy re-entered the building and soared happily upward to the dentist's office. Bruno plumped himself into the chair. "Got it!" he announced.

The dentist swabbed out the place in Bruno's mouth where the tooth used to live. He was laughing so hard he could scarcely steady his fingers. He shook as he cleaned the rescued tooth and dropped it into a small bottle of alcohol. "The tooth that flew out of the window," he roared, handing the corked bottle to Bruno's proud sister.

Out on the street, Bruno began to swagger. "Up all hands. Rise and shine!" he cried, taking long steps. Cristy had a time keeping up.

"You're a good kid, Mosquito Boat." Bruno's voice was warm with gratitude. "I'll certainly do something nice for you some time."

In front of the Angel Flats, Momma and Nick were anxiously awaiting Bruno's return. When they saw him rolling jauntily toward them instead of being borne home on a stretcher, they began to laugh with relief. Cristy displayed the tooth-in-a-bottle.

"I thought it would be a whopper!" exclaimed Nick. "But it's little." After all the toothy hubbub Bruno had made—*this trifle!*

"It's smaller than it felt in my mouth," Bruno admitted.

"Momma, where is Dory?" inquired Cristy. She was suddenly weary of dental doings.

"Mrs. Harlovich, the good kind body, is keeping him," answered Momma, as she preceded her children up the stairs. "That makes me think, Cristina," she continued. "Your poppa says okay about Dory, if we make sure nothing happens to him in traffic. Next Monday, my girl, your own momma will carry the precious bambino to Baby Care school."

On the steps behind Momma, Bruno pinched Cristy's elbow. When she turned to look at him, he winked. But she was filled with too great a joy to remember his forecast that Momma would give in. At last, after all the dreaming and planning, there remained but one big IF. Now the final answer depended on Cristy's classmates—"yes" or "no" for Dory.

The junior class in Baby Care assembled for its sixth lesson. There was a different baby. Cristy regarded him with affection, but she knew as well as she knew anything that he could not compare with Dory. Today her thoughts were all for Dory. When would Nurse Downing ask the girls the fateful question? The moments were passing. The hour was almost up.

"You did quite well today." Nurse was praising Marie. "You may be the one to carry the baby back to the nursery. But wait! Before I dismiss the class—Cristina Romano has asked to bring her baby brother to model in our final practice next Monday. I have given her my permission, if it is all right with the rest of you. What about it?"

Cristy wouldn't allow herself to look at anyone. But behind her Ann O'Bannon spoke up. "It's okay with me." Ann giggled. As she had so truly said on the Reed's pond that day, Cristy Romano was always *going* for something odd.

Eight other giggling voices echoed Ann's consent.

"And you, Marie?" asked the nurse.

Over the baby in her arms, Marie gave Cristy a cool, grown-up look. "I think it's wacky," declared Marie. "Who would care to lug a heavy baby all the way to Dexter House? Not me!"

The other girls laughed, a little embarrassed, yet rather admiring Marie's hard-boiled manner. Cristy let out the breath she had been holding, and with it a flutter of laughter. Not the same kind. *Boy!*

On the street outside Dexter House, the girls who did not live on Finney Street gave Cristy a good-bye which warmed her heart. "So long, Cristy," they said. "We can't wait to see your baby brother. He'd better be good!" And while Marie, Bertha and Ann could not resist making a little fun of Cristy at the doors of Angel Flats, they were good-humored. "See you Monday, Cristy."

Now! To tell Momma! To whisper the glad tidings into Dory's ear! Cristy had bounded halfway up the third flight when she met Nick. He had eaten his lunch and was returning to work. But why was he making such a racket about it?

"Am I glad you came this minute!" yelled Nick. "A letter came. It's from that author woman. I want to know what she says." Nick turned. He tore up the stairs with Cristy.

The letter was propped against the tumbler at Cristy's place, laid for the noon meal. Momma was all smiles.

"Open it, Cristy! Read it!" ordered Nick. "I haven't got all day."

Bruno, coming in just then from a morning of monkeyshines, had to know what all the excitement was about. While Momma explained, and Nick urged haste, Cristy ran the edge of her table knife under the flap of the envelope. She would have liked to fly to some hiding place where she might read the letter to herself, and gloat and dream over it. But Nick was breathing down her neck. He finished the letter, rapidly.

"Doesn't know any horse, for Pete's sake!" With these scornful words Nick dismissed the author from his mind. He dashed out of the door and back to the fruit-and-vegetable stand.

Breathlessly, Cristy read the letter aloud to Momma and Bruno.

"Dear Loving Reader (as you signed yourself). I am glad that my books give you a 'nice feeling inside.' Perhaps that is because I, too, have 'feelings' as I plan and write. No, I have never written any horse stories. An author must write of things she knows about, and I do not know horses. Your letter, Cristina, is one of the nicest I have ever received, because you told me what is in your heart and mind. I shall think of you as a true book lover. Even though a book may fall to pieces and nothing is left of cover, pages and shape, it is never lost to the one who has loved it. I hope that your life shall always be made more rich and happy because good books are wonderful to you. They are very wonderful to me, also. Your friend, Deborah Bruce."

" 'Friend'!" breathed Cristy. "She's my friend. Oh, Mom!"

17. DORY'S BIG DAY

*E*VEN in drab and crowded Number Fifty-One, Monday dawned bright as gold for Cristy Romano. Momma complained of the heat. After breakfast, as she padded around the flat in her bare feet, she stubbed a toe against a chair leg. She collapsed in pain. In no time the toe was blue and swollen.

"Oh, Cristina-girl!" moaned Momma. "Such a bad thing to happen! Never could I stump down stairs and to Dexter House carrying the bambino. What to do—is—is *nothing!*"

Cristy heated water. She poured it into a basin, which Bruno placed on the floor by Momma's chair. Momma soaked her burning toe, while Cristy wept for her. But oh, the tears were also for the ruin of Dory's big day at Dexter House!

"Don't worry, Momma." Cristy made herself stop crying. But over the heating of more water, she lifted pleading eyes to Bruno.

"Sorry, Mosquito Boat." Bruno did indeed look very troubled. "I'd carry the little cargo to Dexter House in a minute, only I've got this date with my old boyhood pal. I haven't even seen the guy yet. We're going on a toot in his jalopy and take a couple of girls. I couldn't let them down at this late date."

"On account of his tooth, Bruno's not had fun yet with people his age," explained Momma. "Bruno, please go to drugstore. Phone doctor. Ask him to come. But he can't work a miracle, Cristina. I still couldn't hobble out."

While Bruno was away, Cristy made timid suggestions. "Maybe Nick and I could take turns carrying Dory."

Momma shook her head. "Poppa wouldn't like. Wiggsy-lady said the one who carries Dory five blocks must be strong body."

"There's Mrs. Harlovich." Cristy tried this without much hope.

"Mrs. Harlovich doesn't go on street often. She's not young any more." Momma flinched at a fresh stab of pain. "Sooner than ask her to carry Dory all that way, I'd limp out on this bad toe and faint in front of Muggsy's Grill. Never a single body in Angel Flats would I ask. It would raise talk. The women would say, 'Did you hear how Mrs. Romano sends her baby to Dexter House for washing?' "

"Poppa—"

"Phone for Poppa? Poppa leave his job?" cried Momma. "Girl, think where our bread and meat comes from, and the roof over our heads! Lovey, my heart aches for you as bad as toe aches. But now you take brave breath. Go to Baby Care school the same as every week. Want the girls to see your eyes all red? Of course not! Run to Mrs. Harlovich, now. Ask if she will kindly stay with your momma while you and Bruno are both gone. When school is over, hurry home and be the best helper and trained nurse your momma and little Salvadore ever had."

Cristy had no more than crept sadly outside Number Fifty-One when Bruno's head and shoulders appeared in the stair well. "Ahoy, Mosquito Boat," he sang out, cheerfully. "About ship. You're on the wrong tack." He guided Cristy back into the flat.

"Steady as you go, Mom!" he breezed. "Doc will be here within the hour. While I was glued to the phone in the drug-store booth, I called Bud. I said I'd go on the toot some other day. I said we'd had an accident in the family, and so we have, poor Mom! But there was no need gassing to Bud that if I don't jib around and take Dory to Dexter House, my sister will pile up on the rocks. Clear for action, Cristy. Make the little cargo waterproof. We're bound for the high seas."

Grinning, Bruno made his smartest hand salute. "I couldn't let this day drop a dud on Mosquito Boat, after all she did for me the time my tooth was yanked out."

The flat seemed to shimmer and spin, with Bruno sending out beams of blessing. Cristy rushed forward to throw her arms around him.

"My Bruno!" cried Momma. "In the great Book of Life Saint Peter writes down good marks for Bruno Torelli!"

Bruno blinked, trying not to appear too pleased with himself.

Within twenty minutes Mrs. Harlovich had taken charge of Momma. Cristy and Bruno were headed east on Finney Street. The bambino, large-eyed, content, and mostly bare, was perched plumply in the crook of Bruno's arm. "Shipshape, that's us," Bruno boasted. He had put on his dress whites. He was dazzled by his own dapper appearance. Cristy was dazzled to walk beside him. There had been little time for any real primping on her part. She had whisked a washcloth over herself and Dory, pinned him up freshly, brushed her hair, and donned a clean skirt and blouse. In her hand she carried a paper bag containing articles necessary for Dory.

"We've time to burn," Bruno remarked. "So we'll cruise along at about five knots, greeting our friends and making everybody happy." Surely everyone in the world must be happy on this day of days, when Cristy Romano was simply dizzy with joy. And five knots' speed limit was enough for anyone so breathless.

"We'll drop anchor and go ashore here," Bruno announced. He turned into the Chinese laundry. Chin Ying could not read

English very well, but he could read Bruno like a book. His narrow eyes glittered with amusement.

"Velly pletty baby," he said. "Velly nice saila suit. Chin Ying wash that suit velly fine some day soon."

"Not a speck on it so far," answered Bruno, uneasily. He stayed only long enough to make sure that Chin Ying got an eyeful of handsome Navy man with handsome baby.

Hailing from shipboard was enough at Ciello's. "Gee!" exclaimed Nick, gazing at Bruno's dress whites, "I wish I could go as far as Dexter House with you."

Bruno dipped a salute at Muggsy's Grill. In fact, he dropped anchor and stayed quite a while. He had a hard time getting under way again, for the waitresses crowded around, fluttering their eyelashes at him and gushing over Dory.

"Maybe we had better go faster than five knots," Cristy suggested. "I wonder what time it is by now."

"Don't worry, Mosquito Boat," Bruno assured Cristy. "I'll have you and the little cargo moored at Dexter House in time. But it's plenty hot today, and Dory steaming on my arm like a boiler. Makes me thirsty."

The fleet had now reached St. James Street. It was coasting past Mike's Coke Bar, when Bruno stopped so suddenly that Cristy bumped into him. The bar was open to the street. Bruno plumped Dory on the counter, which was shaded and cooled by an awning. "Couple of Cokes, Mike," ordered Bruno.

Cristy was thirsty, but not so much that she wanted to waste minutes drinking a Coke. "What time is it?" she inquired of Mike.

"Ten minutes of ten," answered Mike, glancing at his wrist watch.

Cristy almost strangled. "Did you hear that, Bruno?" she cried. "I'm due at ten."

"Pipe down, kid." Bruno's smile was sunny. "We're less than a block and a half from Dexter House."

"Who's the little guy?" asked Mike, pleased with Dory's liquid eyes and rosy morning charm.

"Kid brother," answered Bruno, proudly.

"My treat, then, on account of the little guy." Mike shoved Bruno's coins back to him.

Expressing thanks, Bruno was about to scoop Dory to his arm again, when a pretty girl appeared at the bar.

"Strike my colors! Judy Grace, of all people!" cried Bruno. "I haven't seen you since our high-school days." Bruno made high school sound like long, long ago. Judy Grace uttered squeals of surprise and delight. She and Bruno launched into streams of talk and merry banter. It was as if they had all day, and were the only two in the world. Cristy and Dory seemed utterly forgotten.

By now it was surely ten o'clock, or more. Even if she could leave this minute, Cristy would be late. Miss Downing, Miss Pat and Wiggsy would be worrying. The junior class would be seated and waiting. Nurse would give up and get a baby from the day nursery. Darling Dory would lose out! Anger and despair boiled up within Cristy. With sharp fingernails she clawed at Bruno's hands. She tugged furiously at his jumper. "Bruno, give Dory to me! Give him to me this minute! I'll carry him. Don't you see I'm late? Don't you see you're spoiling everything for Dory? Oh-hh, *you!*"

Bruno jumped. All at once he saw the day again through Cristy's eyes. "Full speed ahead, Sis!" he cried. "Let's go!"

And without a parting word for Judy Grace, Bruno swept Dory off the bar, and leaped toward the Avenue.

At the Dexter House entrance Miss Pat and Nurse Downing were anxiously scanning the street. They rushed down the steps. Nurse reached for Dory. Miss Pat took Cristy's hand. "You will come back at eleven?" she asked Bruno. She did not even glance at his natty uniform. He was only Cristy's strong half brother, of some use today.

"I'll be here, Miss," promised Bruno, meekly.

Wiggsy was waiting grimly outside her office. When she saw Cristy, she barked out, "Thank Heaven," and closed the door.

In the washroom Cristy's pent-up nervous tears overflowed into the basin, into the paper towel, into Miss Pat's embrace. "Bruno stopped everywhere," she wept.

"Cheer up, Cristy. You're here, in the nick of time."

At the classroom door Cristy's glance flew ahead of the juniors to Dory. He was seated on the enamel topped table. It was certainly hunky-dory to have all his clothes off. The hand of this starchy lady in white was firm and dependable against his back. How jolly to see ten young faces smiling and nodding at him! *Oops*, there was a familiar one—Cristy! Dory's round, ringleted head bobbed with mirth. He curled his toes and showed his one pearly tooth.

Cristina slipped into her chair with a long sigh of relief. Peace flowed through her.

"This is young Salvadore Romano," began Nurse Downing. "As today's lesson is our final one with a baby as model, I will quiz you as I go through the routine myself."

But so very busy did Master Salvadore keep the nurse that she scarcely had time for quizzing. He had her and all the girls chuckling. For every chuckle he crowed, sociably. He slapped his bath water into carousing jets that showered everyone. He licked suds with relish. He chewed on the washcloth. He gurgled when he was dried and oiled and pinned and brushed. He took his bottle with pleasure, and bubbled at the proper moment. "Class, this is undoubtedly a loved baby," declared Nurse Downing. She gave a pretty little lecture, repeating, with her eyes on Dory, how love and happy babyhood are related.

Cristy felt floaty enough to soar to the ceiling. Never had truth been spoken more clearly. Oh, getting beloved Dory here had been a great deal of trouble for a good many people! But it had been done, and was worth every bit of the struggle. No matter how many classes in Baby Care might be taught at Dexter House through the years, there could never be a more enchanting model than Salvadore Romano. This was Cristy's own sure, secret, and lovely knowledge.

At the eighth and final lesson the diplomas were awarded, each with its big gold star. *Baby Care. Successfully completed.* Cristina. Ann. Bertha. Marie.

Poppa was proud. He took Cristy to the second-hand shop to get a frame for the diploma. The dusty old owner of the shop poked among piles of junk. He found something which Poppa said would do, when cleaned and painted. To make sure, Poppa held the diploma loosely within the frame, to try it. The second-hand man peered around at Cristy. "Can you frame a star?" he asked, in a dry whisper.

Cristy didn't know what to say. The question was as queer as the old man himself. But it was plain, as he nodded and twinkled, that he believed Cristy could indeed "frame a star."

18 . JOY

*I*F anyone had told Cristy at the close of school that it would take her all summer to read ten books, she would not have believed it.

"Very busy summer for my Cristina," said Momma. "How many stars shine for you in library now?"

"One more book read, and I shall have ten stars on the big poster," answered Cristy. "Momma, Mrs. Rozell is going to have a story hour for all the boys and girls who win stars. It will be held just before school opens."

"Soon school opens. Soon my Bruno goes to ship." Momma looked sad. . . . "Bruno, are you sure to have a ride in your buddy's jalopy to bring Carlotta home?"

"All set, Mom." Bruno patted her shoulder. "Bud and I are going tomorrow. I hope Cristy has written to the Todds, with a hint for an extra chicken in the fryer." Bruno winked.

"I did write, but not about the chicken." Cristy laughed. "I said you'd be there, and I told Mrs. Eva I'd had a letter from Deborah Bruce. I thanked her and Daddy George for being so good to all of us."

"Todds are fine people." Momma was quick to say it. "And tomorrow our Lotta, home again!" The Romanos could scarcely wait to see Carlotta.

Bruno had managed a little talk with Mr. Ciello, as delightful as the fruit man had enjoyed in a dog's age. And on Saturday, which was one of Mr. Ciello's busiest days, he found himself carrying on without Nick Romano. For by that time the boy was riding with Bruno and his buddy to Caspar County. Nick was packed with a silent joy. He had not been with Bruno nearly as much as he wanted to be. And there was Old-Timer on the Todd farm! Nick's hand itched for the grooming brush. He could scarcely wait for the velvety tickle of Old-Timer's nose against his ear.

When Carlotta came home with her brothers that evening, her eyes sparkled above the huge bouquet she held in a funnel of dampened paper. "Little giant pink frills," late roses, daylilies, zinnias and gladioli—how Carlotta's hands treasured them!

Mrs. Eva had sent Momma a dressed hen, a basket of ripe tomatoes, and a bag of snap beans.

Nick stammered over a piece of news. "Mr. Todd would like for me to spend the whole summer on the farm next year. I can help with the work the same as Charles Westover, once I've learned. I can help take care of—" Nick couldn't quite finish it.

"The horse?" coaxed Cristy.

"Yes. Old-Timer," gulped Nick.

"The farm is wonderful," Bruno declared. "Never saw such a lot of whopper hogs. But between a farm and the sea, I say 'all aboard that's going aboard.'" And Bruno Torelli, seaman, swaggered away from Number Fifty-One to join his ship.

Cristy reported on her tenth book on Tuesday of the final week of vacation. Mrs. Rozell pasted the tenth star on the poster after Cristy's name. She told Cristy that she had been able to arrange something much nicer than the Friday story hour. "Be sure to come. You especially, Cristy, must be here."

"Why?" asked Cristy.

"Because." Mrs. Rozell laughed.

When Cristy paid Dexter House a brief call, she told Miss Pat what the librarian had said. "I know all about it," teased Miss Pat, "but you can't pry the secret out of me. I'd give a good deal to see your face when you go to that library party on Friday. But I'm off on a vacation tomorrow."

"You will come back to Dexter House?"

"I think so. Be happy, Cristy Romano."

Early Friday afternoon Cristy enjoyed a swim in the Dexter House pool. It was the best—well, the only way to get an all-over bath. At home again, she donned the good dress which she had proudly taken to the Todd farm before she knew it had not been furnished by someone named So-She-Ate-Cherries. Clean and brushed, Cristy skipped down the four flights.

"Party at the library at four o'clock!" she caroled, meeting Ann O'Bannon at the second floor. "It's for us who have read ten books."

"You and your library books!" Ann laughed. She didn't give a hoot for books. Cristy didn't give a hoot if Ann laughed, either. "Ann and Bertha and Marie just don't know what they're missing, that's all," thought Cristy. Her skipping feet lifted as lightly as wings. Joy in books can make a booklover feel blessed from head to toe.

Almost all of the gold-starred readers had come to the party. Mrs. Rozell was wearing a dress which Cristy had never seen before. She was flushed and smiling as she straightened rows of chairs for the children. It was ten minutes after four.

"I have a surprise for you this afternoon, children," announced Mrs. Rozell. "I happened to hear that a certain person is spending a few days in our city. Although I had never met her, I telephoned to her. I asked if she would come and help us celebrate the end of our summer reading adventure. She agreed. Children, I am sure that none of you has ever seen a real, live author. So I'm happy to introduce Miss Deborah Bruce, whose books many of you have read."

A strong breeze from high heaven seemed to blow over and among the seated children. It set them to bouncing. It stirred up "oh's" and "ah's," both soft and loud. For a dizzy moment it seemed to spin Cristy Romano around like the wind-spun weathercock on the Todd barn in Caspar County. She was no more vocal than a weathercock, either. She could not have said a word.

A tall woman whom no child had noticed came out from behind the circulation desk. It was Deborah Bruce. She stood smiling down into the young upturned faces. She was quietly dressed. She was not beautiful. But her eyes were both thoughtful and merry, as if she were half grown up, half child. The lines around her mouth were laughter lines. The little frown between her brows had come from thinking so deeply over her stories, thought by thought, word by word, sentence by sentence.

Cristy sat in a trance of delight, listening to Deborah Bruce talk about her own childhood and her lifelong reading adventures. "One cannot be a writer unless she is first a reader," declared Deborah Bruce. She told the children about her present home, her cat and her dog. "Children ask me if I am married, and how many children I have. But, no, I am not married. Yet I have many children. They are the boys and girls who live in my books." Cristy and the others thought this was a clever thing to say. And how true! The author named her fourteen books. She inquired if any had read them. Cristy's hand shot up eleven times.

Miss Bruce told her audience that she was humbly thankful

for the talent which had been given her. "I would rather write one lasting book for children than to write many books for grown-ups," she earnestly avowed.

"Oh, she's our very own author! She belongs to us!" rejoiced Cristy to herself.

The author then pointed to the big book poster. "The ten gold stars each of you has won are only of paper. But they stand for

something very real. Each star means that a book you have loved enough to remember shall for a long time be a bright star in your mind."

Momma had said it a little differently, and very surprisingly. Perhaps it was what the dusty old second-hand man had meant, in a way, when he had asked Cristy if she could frame a star?

The children crowded up to thrust little scraps of paper at the author, clamoring for autographs. But Cristy hung back, shyly waiting. Would she have the courage to speak? Would she dare to remind Deborah Bruce that they had exchanged letters? "Maybe you remember." Cristy might say it.

But a moment later, while the children stood thick around the author, Cristy found herself in the "library work room," as Mrs. Rozell called it. The librarian had beckoned Cristy in. Amid a good deal of book clutter, a small table had been spread with a linen cloth. There was a china teapot, cups and saucers, plates of cakes and candy mints. Water steamed in a kettle over an electric grill. Cristy stared. Was it for a party?

Mrs. Rozell held out a package. She explained to Cristy. "Pat Logan left a gift for you. I called you in because I do not want the other children to know, and to feel left out. Please open the package."

Cristy managed to untie the bow without spoiling the pretty ribbon. She was careful not to tear the gay paper. *Glory,* a book! It was the book which Cristy had read at the farm, lying on her stomach because her back was sore from being swept off a horse that silly morning. It was "the most outstandingest book," by Cristy's favorite author, Deborah Bruce! Cristy couldn't speak. There were no words. How good, oh, how kind and understanding of Miss Pat to give Cristy the present she would rather have above all others—a book—*the* book! How much better than anything So-She-Ate-Cherries might ever have done!

Wonders to tell, Cristy stayed for the party in the library work room! She was invited! Much of the talk between Mrs. Rozell and Miss Bruce was over her head, but it was bliss to sit there and listen. And presently Cristy was kindly questioned. Who would have dreamed that she would be telling about Dory and Baby Care, Momma and the other Romanos? Who would have dreamed that Miss Bruce would be so interested?

"I remembered your name, Cristina," she declared, "because it is unusual, and because your letter was so nice. I'm keeping it. Fancy meeting you, when I never expected to!"

She wrote in Cristy's book: "Autographed for Cristina Romano, with the hope that she shall always be a reader both loving and adventurous. Deborah Bruce."

Cristy wanted to cry and she wanted to laugh, which is a dangerous mixture of feeling. So she laughed with the author and Mrs. Rozell.

Suddenly she heard Nick's voice. He was inquiring for her at the desk in the main room. When she went toward him, he scowled, saying that Momma had sent him, and why had she stayed until almost dark? Indeed the days were growing shorter. Beyond the library entrance Cristy could see that dusk was gathering on Finney Street.

"I stayed for a party, Nick! We had grown-up tea and little cakes. Here! I saved a cooky for you. Nick, you will never believe! Look who's coming out of the workroom. It's the author, Deborah Bruce!"

Nick turned fiery red. Shifting his cooky with awkward haste, he allowed his hand to be taken by Miss Bruce, but for no more than a second. "I'll tell you something," he said to her, earnestly. "If you knew the horse that I know, you'd write a big book about him!"

Hasty good-byes were exchanged. On the library steps Cristy had to show Nick her book with its autograph. "Gee whiz!" exclaimed Nick. "Holy Smoke!" He was really impressed.

"I can't wait to show Momma and Poppa, and explain to Carlotta!" Cristy jumped to the sidewalk.

"Come along, then, or Mom will be sending the cops after us."

Sister and brother walked along Finney Street. "Look, Cristy!" Nick pointed upward. "Remember I said there was a star over Muggsy's Grill? I haven't noticed it all summer. But this evening, there it is! Now make a funnel of your hand, and look through the opening, like this."

"Yes, I see it," answered Cristy. "It twinkles like the stars over the Todd farm. It's real. It makes me glad."

Cristy held her book carefully, lovingly. "Summer adventure," she thought. Aloud she said, " 'Star light, star bright.' Nick, I don't need to make a single wish this evening. Not after such a rich and wonderful summer!"

Above Muggsy's Grill and Finney Street the little star twinkled. Far away, and faintly, it shone above Cristy Romano's world.

THE END

Books by Mabel Leigh Hunt:

Beggar's Daughter
Cupola House
Cristy at Skippinghills
Stars for Cristy
Miss Jellytot's Visit
Singing Among Strangers
Ladycake Farm
Better Known as Johnny Appleseed
The Double Birthday Present
"Have You Seen Tom Thumb?"
Benjie's Hat
Little Girl with Seven Names